Love and Other Happy Endings

Love and Other Happy Endings

A Collection of Classic Short Stories

Edited By

M. R. Nelson

AnnorlundaBooks

Published in the United States by Annorlunda Books.

Queries: info@annorlundaenterprises.com.

First edition.

ISBN: 978-1-944354-03-9

Contents

Introduction

This is the second "taster flight" of classic short stories I've assembled. The first was a collection of love stories with a hint of the one who got away, called *Missed Chances*. In this flight, I again focus on love, but this time on the happy ending. Don't be fooled into thinking these stories will be less complex, though. As it turns out, happy endings come in a lot of different guises.

Just as a taster flight of wine or craft beer allows you to sample a wider range of drinks than you could if you were drinking full-size glasses, this taster flight of stories allows you to sample the styles and ideas of more authors. A nice side benefit of wine and beer taster flights is that often by comparing the samples to each other, you notice characteristics you would have otherwise missed. I think the same is true for taster flights of short stories: By reading these stories together, I hope you'll notice aspects of the individual stories that might not stand out when the stories are read on their own.

We usually think of romance when we think of a "happy ending," and that is certainly reflected in this collection. There are, of course, other ways to have a happy ending, and the stories in this collection at least hint at that, too. I don't want to spoil any of the stories by discussing why I selected them before you read them, so I've put a short afterword at the end of this book, in which I explain why I chose the stories and provide a little bit of background on each.

Enjoy the flight!

The Singing Lesson
By Katherine Mansfield

With despair—cold, sharp despair—buried deep in her heart like a wicked knife, Miss Meadows, in cap and gown and carrying a little baton, trod the cold corridors that led to the music hall. Girls of all ages, rosy from the air, and bubbling over with that gleeful excitement that comes from running to school on a fine autumn morning, hurried, skipped, fluttered by; from the hollow class-rooms came a quick drumming of voices; a bell rang; a voice like a bird cried, "Muriel." And then there came from the staircase a tremendous knock-knock-knocking. Some one had dropped her dumbbells.

The Science Mistress stopped Miss Meadows.

"Good morning," she cried, in her sweet, affected drawl. "Isn't it cold? It might be win-ter."

Miss Meadows, hugging the knife, stared in hatred at the Science Mistress. Everything about her was sweet, pale, like honey. You would not have been surprised to see a bee caught in the tangles of that yellow hair.

"It is rather sharp," said Miss Meadows, grimly.

The other smiled her sugary smile.

"You look fro-zen," said she. Her blue eyes opened wide; there came a mocking light in them. (Had she noticed anything?)

"Oh, not quite as bad as that," said Miss Meadows, and she gave the Science Mistress, in exchange for her smile, a quick grimace and passed on...

Forms Four, Five, and Six were assembled in the music hall. The noise was deafening. On the platform, by the piano, stood Mary Beazley, Miss Meadows' favourite, who played accompaniments. She was turning the music stool. When she saw Miss Meadows she gave a loud, warning "Sh-sh! girls!" and Miss

Meadows, her hands thrust in her sleeves, the baton under her arm, strode down the centre aisle, mounted the steps, turned sharply, seized the brass music stand, planted it in front of her, and gave two sharp taps with her baton for silence.

"Silence, please! Immediately!" and, looking at nobody, her glance swept over that sea of coloured flannel blouses, with bobbing pink faces and hands, quivering butterfly hair-bows, and music-books outspread. She knew perfectly well what they were thinking. "Meady is in a wax." Well, let them think it! Her eyelids quivered; she tossed her head, defying them. What could the thoughts of those creatures matter to some one who stood there bleeding to death, pierced to the heart, to the heart, by such a letter—

... "I feel more and more strongly that our marriage would be a mistake. Not that I do not love you. I love you as much as it is possible for me to love any woman, but, truth to tell, I have come to the conclusion that I am not a marrying man, and the idea of settling down fills me with nothing but—" and the word "disgust" was scratched out lightly and "regret" written over the top.

Basil! Miss Meadows stalked over to the piano. And Mary Beazley, who was waiting for this moment, bent forward; her curls fell over her cheeks while she breathed, "Good morning, Miss Meadows," and she motioned towards rather than handed to her mistress a beautiful yellow chrysanthemum. This little ritual of the flower had been gone through for ages and ages, quite a term and a half. It was as much part of the lesson as opening the piano. But this morning, instead of taking it up, instead of tucking it into her belt while she leant over Mary and said, "Thank you, Mary. How very nice! Turn to page thirty-two," what was Mary's horror when Miss Meadows totally ignored the chrysanthemum, made no reply to her greeting, but said in a voice of ice, "Page fourteen, please, and mark the accents well."

Staggering moment! Mary blushed until the tears stood in her eyes, but Miss Meadows was gone back to the music stand; her voice rang through the music hall.

"Page fourteen. We will begin with page fourteen. 'A Lament.' Now, girls, you ought to know it by this time. We shall take it all together; not in parts, all together. And without expression. Sing it, though, quite simply, beating time with the left hand."

She raised the baton; she tapped the music stand twice. Down came Mary on the opening chord; down came all those left hands, beating the air, and in chimed those young, mournful voices:—

"Fast! Ah, too Fast Fade the Ro-o-ses of Pleasure;
Soon Autumn yields unto Wi-i-nter Drear.
Fleetly! Ah, Fleetly Mu-u-sic's Gay Measure
Passes away from the Listening Ear."

Good Heavens, what could be more tragic than that lament! Every note was a sigh, a sob, a groan of awful mournfulness. Miss Meadows lifted her arms in the wide gown and began conducting with both hands. "...I feel more and more strongly that our marriage would be a mistake..." she beat. And the voices cried: "Fleetly! Ah, Fleetly." What could have possessed him to write such a letter! What could have led up to it! It came out of nothing. His last letter had been all about a fumed-oak bookcase he had bought for "our" books, and a "natty little hall-stand" he had seen, "a very neat affair with a carved owl on a bracket, holding three hat-brushes in its claws." How she had smiled at that! So like a man to think one needed three hat-brushes! "From the Listening Ear," sang the voices.

"Once again," said Miss Meadows. "But this time in parts. Still without expression." "Fast! Ah, too Fast." With the gloom of the contraltos added, one could scarcely help shuddering. "Fade the Roses of Pleasure." Last time he had come to see her, Basil had worn a rose in his buttonhole. How handsome he had looked in that bright blue suit, with that dark red rose! And he knew it, too. He couldn't help knowing it. First he stroked his hair, then his moustache; his teeth gleamed when he smiled.

"The headmaster's wife keeps on asking me to dinner. It's a perfect nuisance. I never get an evening to myself in that place."

"But can't you refuse?"

"Oh, well, it doesn't do for a man in my position to be unpopular."

"Music's Gay Measure," wailed the voices. The willow trees, outside the high, narrow windows, waved in the wind. They had lost half their leaves. The tiny ones that clung wriggled like fishes caught on a line. "...I am not a marrying man..." The voices were silent; the piano waited.

"Quite good," said Miss Meadows, but still in such a strange, stony tone that the younger girls began to feel positively frightened. "But now that we know it, we shall take it with expression. As much expression as you can put into it. Think of the words, girls. Use your imaginations. 'Fast! Ah, too Fast,'" cried Miss Meadows. "That ought to break out—a loud, strong forte—a lament. And then in the second line, 'Winter Drear,' make that 'Drear' sound as if a cold wind were blowing through it. 'Dre-ear!'" said she so awfully that Mary Beazley, on the music stool, wriggled her spine. "The third line should be one crescendo. 'Fleetly! Ah, Fleetly Music's Gay Measure.' Breaking on the first word of the last line, 'Passes.' And then on the word, 'Away,' you must begin to die... to fade... until 'The Listening Ear' is nothing more than a faint whisper... You can slow down as much as you like almost on the last line. Now, please."

Again the two light taps; she lifted her arms again. 'Fast! Ah, too Fast.' "... and the idea of settling down fills me with nothing but disgust—" Disgust was what he had written. That was as good as to say their engagement was definitely broken off. Broken off! Their engagement! People had been surprised enough that she had got engaged. The Science Mistress would not believe it at first. But nobody had been as surprised as she. She was thirty. Basil was twenty-five. It had been a miracle, simply a miracle, to hear him say, as they walked home from church that very dark night, "You know, somehow or other, I've got fond of you." And he had taken hold of the end of her ostrich feather boa. "Passes away from the Listening Ear."

"Repeat! Repeat!" said Miss Meadows. "More expression, girls! Once more!"

"Fast! Ah, too Fast." The older girls were crimson; some of the younger ones began to cry. Big spots of rain blew against the windows, and one could hear the willows whispering, "...not that I do not love you..."

"But, my darling, if you love me," thought Miss Meadows, "I don't mind how much it is. Love me as little as you like." But she knew he didn't love her. Not to have cared enough to scratch out that word "disgust," so that she couldn't read it! "Soon Autumn yields unto Winter Drear." She would have to leave the school, too. She could never face the Science Mistress or the girls after it got known. She would have to disappear somewhere. "Passes away." The voices began to die, to fade, to whisper... to vanish...

Suddenly the door opened. A little girl in blue walked fussily up the aisle, hanging her head, biting her lips, and twisting the silver bangle on her red little wrist. She came up the steps and stood before Miss Meadows.

"Well, Monica, what is it?"

"Oh, if you please, Miss Meadows," said the little girl, gasping, "Miss Wyatt wants to see you in the mistress's room."

"Very well," said Miss Meadows. And she called to the girls, "I shall put you on your honour to talk quietly while I am away." But they were too subdued to do anything else. Most of them were blowing their noses.

The corridors were silent and cold; they echoed to Miss Meadows' steps. The head mistress sat at her desk. For a moment she did not look up. She was as usual disentangling her eyeglasses, which had got caught in her lace tie. "Sit down, Miss Meadows," she said very kindly. And then she picked up a pink envelope from the blotting-pad. "I sent for you just now because this telegram has come for you."

"A telegram for me, Miss Wyatt?"

Basil! He had committed suicide, decided Miss Meadows. Her hand flew out, but Miss Wyatt held the telegram back a moment. "I hope it's not bad news," she said, so more than kindly. And Miss Meadows tore it open.

"Pay no attention to letter, must have been mad, bought hat-stand to-day—Basil," she read. She couldn't take her eyes off the telegram.

"I do hope it's nothing very serious," said Miss Wyatt, leaning forward.

"Oh, no, thank you, Miss Wyatt," blushed Miss Meadows. "It's nothing bad at all. It's"—and she gave an apologetic little laugh—"it's from my fiancé saying that... saying that—" There was a pause. "I see," said Miss Wyatt. And another pause. Then—"You've fifteen minutes more of your class, Miss Meadows, haven't you?"

"Yes, Miss Wyatt." She got up. She half ran towards the door.

"Oh, just one minute, Miss Meadows," said Miss Wyatt. "I must say I don't approve of my teachers having telegrams sent to them in school hours, unless in case of very bad news, such as death," explained Miss Wyatt, "or a very serious accident, or something to that effect. Good news, Miss Meadows, will always keep, you know."

On the wings of hope, of love, of joy, Miss Meadows sped back to the music hall, up the aisle, up the steps, over to the piano.

"Page thirty-two, Mary," she said, "page thirty-two," and, picking up the yellow chrysanthemum, she held it to her lips to hide her smile. Then she turned to the girls, rapped with her baton: "Page thirty-two, girls. Page thirty-two."

"We come here To-day with Flowers o'erladen,
With Baskets of Fruit and Ribbons to boot,
To-oo Congratulate..."

"Stop! Stop!" cried Miss Meadows. "This is awful. This is dreadful." And she beamed at her girls. "What's the matter with you all? Think, girls, think of what you're singing. Use your imaginations. 'With Flowers o'erladen. Baskets of Fruit and Ribbons to boot.' And 'Congratulate.'" Miss Meadows broke off. "Don't look so doleful, girls. It ought to sound warm, joyful, eager. 'Congratulate.' Once more. Quickly. All together. Now then!"

And this time Miss Meadows' voice sounded over all the other voices—full, deep, glowing with expression.

Akin to Love
By L.M. Montgomery

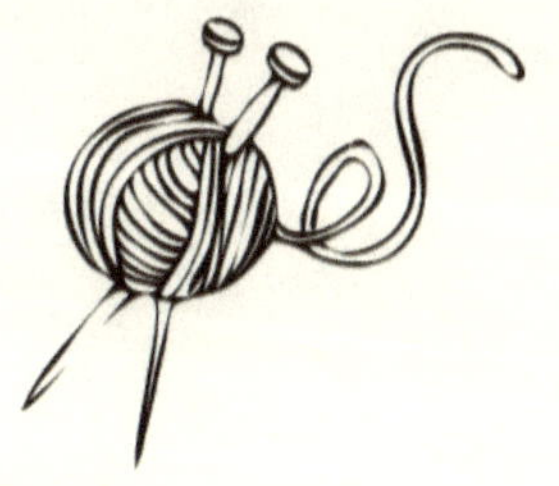

Akin to Love

David Hartley had dropped in to pay a neighbourly call on Josephine Elliott. It was well along in the afternoon, and outside, in the clear crispness of a Canadian winter, the long blue shadows from the tall firs behind the house were falling over the snow.

It was a frosty day, and all the windows of every room where there was no fire were covered with silver palms. But the big, bright kitchen was warm and cosy, and somehow seemed to David more tempting than ever before, and that is saying a good deal. He had an uneasy feeling that he had stayed long enough and ought to go. Josephine was knitting at a long gray sock with doubly aggressive energy, and that was a sign that she was talked out. As long as Josephine had plenty to say, her plump white fingers, where her mother's wedding ring was lost in dimples, moved slowly among her needles. When conversation flagged she fell to her work as furiously as if a husband and half a dozen sons were waiting for its completion. David often wondered in his secret soul what Josephine did with all the interminable gray socks she knitted. Sometimes he concluded that she put them in the home missionary barrels; again, that she sold them to her hired man. At any rate, they were very warm and comfortable looking, and David sighed as he thought of the deplorable state his own socks were generally in.

When David sighed Josephine took alarm. She was afraid David was going to have one of his attacks of foolishness. She must head him off someway, so she rolled up the gray sock, stabbed the big pudgy ball with her needles, and said she guessed she'd get the tea.

David got up.

"Now, you're not going before tea?" said Josephine hospitably. "I'll have it all ready in no time."

"I ought to go home, I s'pose," said David, with the air and tone of a man dallying with a great temptation. "Zillah'll be waiting tea for me; and there's the stock to tend to."

"I guess Zillah won't wait long," said Josephine. She did not intend it at all, but there was a certain scornful ring in her voice. "You must stay. I've a fancy for company to tea."

David sat down again. He looked so pleased that Josephine went down on her knees behind the stove, ostensibly to get a stick of firewood, but really to hide her smile.

"I suppose he's tickled to death to think of getting a good square meal, after the starvation rations Zillah puts him on," she thought.

But Josephine misjudged David just as much as he misjudged her. She had really asked him to stay to tea out of pity, but David thought it was because she was lonesome, and he hailed that as an encouraging sign. And he was not thinking about getting a good meal either, although his dinner had been such a one as only Zillah Hartley could get up. As he leaned back in his cushioned chair and watched Josephine bustling about the kitchen, he was glorying in the fact that he could spend another hour with her, and sit opposite to her at the table while she poured his tea for him and passed him the biscuits, just as if—just as if—

Here Josephine looked straight at him with such intent and stern brown eyes that David felt she must have read his thoughts, and he colored guiltily. But Josephine did not even notice that he was blushing. She had only paused to wonder whether she would bring out cherry or strawberry preserve; and, having decided on the cherry, took her piercing gaze from David without having seen him at all. But he allowed his thoughts no more vagaries.

Josephine set the table with her mother's wedding china. She used it because it was the anniversary of her mother's wedding day, but David thought it was out of compliment to him. And, as he knew quite well that Josephine prized that china beyond all her other earthly possessions, he stroked his smooth-shaven, dimpled chin with the air of a man to whom is offered a very subtly sweet homage.

Josephine whisked in and out of the pantry, and up and down cellar, and with every whisk a new dainty was added to the table. Josephine, as everybody in Meadowby admitted, was past mistress in the noble art of cookery. Once upon a time rash matrons and ambitious young wives had aspired to rival her, but they had long ago realised the vanity of such efforts and dropped comfortably back to second place.

Josephine felt an artist's pride in her table when she set the teapot on its stand and invited David to sit in. There were pink slices of cold tongue, and crisp green pickles and spiced gooseberry, the recipe for which Josephine had invented herself, and which had taken first prize at the Provincial Exhibition for six successive years; there was a lemon pie which was a symphony in gold and silver, biscuits as light and white as snow, and moist, plummy cubes of fruit cake. There was the ruby-tinted cherry preserve, a mound of amber jelly, and, to crown all, steaming cups of tea, in flavour and fragrance unequalled.

And Josephine, too, sitting at the head of the table, with her smooth, glossy crimps of black hair and cheeks as rosy clear as they had been twenty years ago, when she had been a slender slip of girlhood and bashful young David Hartley had looked at her over his hymn-book in prayer-meeting and tramped all the way home a few feet behind her, because he was too shy to go boldly up and ask if he might see her home.

All taken together, what wonder if David lost his head over that tea-table and determined to ask Josephine the same old question once more? It was eighteen years since he had asked it for the first time, and two years since the last. He would try his luck again; Josephine was certainly more gracious than he remembered her to ever have been before.

When the meal was over Josephine cleared the table and washed the dishes. When she had taken a dry towel and sat down by the window to polish her china David understood that his opportunity had come. He moved over and sat down beside her on the sofa by the window.

Outside the sun was setting in a magnificent arch of light and colour over the snow-clad hills and deep blue St. Lawrence gulf. David grasped at the sunset as an introductory factor.

"Isn't that fine, Josephine?" he said admiringly. "It makes me think of that piece of poetry that used to be in the old Fifth Reader when we went to school. D'ye mind how the teacher used to drill us up in it on Friday afternoons? It begun

> 'Slow sinks more lovely ere his race is run
> Along Morea's hills the setting sun.'"

Then David declaimed the whole passage in a sing-song tone, accompanied by a few crude gestures recalled from long-ago school-boy elocution. Josephine knew what was coming. Every time David proposed to her he had begun by reciting poetry. She twirled her towel around the last plate resignedly. If it had to come, the sooner it was over the better. Josephine knew by experience that there was no heading David off, despite his shyness, when he had once got along as far as the poetry.

"But it's going to be for the last time," she said determinedly. "I'm going to settle this question so decidedly to-night that there'll never be a repetition."

When David had finished his quotation he laid his hand on Josephine's plump arm.

"Josephine," he said huskily, "I s'pose you couldn't—could you now?—make up your mind to have me. I wish you would, Josephine—I wish you would. Don't you think you could, Josephine?"

Josephine folded up her towel, crossed her hands on it, and looked her wooer squarely in the eyes.

"David Hartley," she said deliberately, "what makes you go on asking me to marry you every once in a while when I've told you times out of mind that I can't and won't?"

"Because I can't help hoping that you'll change your mind through time," David replied meekly.

"Well, you just listen to me. I will not marry you. That is in the first place. And in the second, this is to be final. It has to be. You are never to ask me this again under any circumstances. If you do I will not answer you—I will not let on I hear you at all; but (and Josephine spoke very slowly and impressively) I will never speak to you again—never. We are good friends now, and I like you real well, and like to have you drop in for a neighbourly chat as often as you wish to, but there'll be an end, short and sudden, to that, if you don't mind what I say."

"Oh, Josephine, ain't that rather hard?" protested David feebly. It seemed terrible to be cut off from all hope with such finality as this.

"I mean every word of it," returned Josephine calmly. "You'd better go home now, David. I always feel as if I'd like to be alone for a spell after a disagreeable experience."

David obeyed sadly and put on his cap and overcoat. Josephine kindly warned him not to slip and break his legs on the porch, because the floor was as icy as anything; and she even lighted a candle and held it up at the kitchen door to guide him safely out. David, as he trudged sorrowfully homeward across the fields, carried with him the mental picture of a plump, sonsy woman, in a trim dress of plum-coloured homespun and ruffled blue-check apron, haloed by candlelight. It was not a very romantic vision, perhaps, but to David it was more beautiful than anything else in the world.

When David was gone Josephine shut the door with a little shiver. She blew out the candle, for it was not yet dark enough to justify artificial light to her thrifty mind. She thought the big, empty house, in which she was the only living thing, was very lonely. It was so still, except for the slow tick of the "grandfather's clock" and the soft purr and crackle of the wood in the stove. Josephine sat down by the window.

"I wish some of the Sentners would run down," she said aloud. "If David hadn't been so ridiculous I'd have got him to stay the evening. He can be good company when he likes—he's real well-read and intelligent. And he must have dismal times at home there with nobody but Zillah."

She looked across the yard to the little house at the other side of it, where her French-Canadian hired man lived, and watched the purple spiral of smoke from its chimney curling up against the crocus sky.

Would she run over and see Mrs. Leon Poirier and her little black-eyed, brown-skinned baby? No, they never knew what to say to each other.

"If 'twasn't so cold I'd go up and see Ida," she said. "As it is, I guess I'd better fall back on my knitting, for I saw Jimmy Sentner's toes sticking through his socks the other day. How setback poor

David did look, to be sure! But I think I've settled that marrying notion of his once for all and I'm glad of it."

She said the same thing next day to Mrs. Tom Sentner, who had come down to help her pick her geese. They were at work in the kitchen with a big tubful of feathers between them, and on the table a row of dead birds, which Leon had killed and brought in. Josephine was enveloped in a shapeless print wrapper, and had an apron tied tightly around her head to keep the down out of her beautiful hair, of which she was rather proud.

"What do you think, Ida?" she said, with a hearty laugh at the recollection. "David Hartley was here to tea last night, and asked me to marry him again. There's a persistent man for you. I can't brag of ever having had many beaux, but I've certainly had my fair share of proposals."

Mrs. Tom did not laugh. Her thin little face, with its faded prettiness, looked as if she never laughed.

"Why won't you marry him?" she said fretfully.

"Why should I?" retorted Josephine. "Tell me that, Ida Sentner."

"Because it is high time you were married," said Mrs. Tom decisively. "I don't believe in women living single. And I don't see what better you can do than take David Hartley."

Josephine looked at her sister with the interested expression of a person who is trying to understand some mental attitude in another which is a standing puzzle to her. Ida's evident wish to see her married always amused Josephine. Ida had married very young and for fifteen years her life had been one of drudgery and ill-health. Tom Sentner was a lazy, shiftless fellow. He neglected his family and was drunk half his time. Meadowby people said that he beat his wife when "on the spree," but Josephine did not believe that, because she did not think that Ida could keep from telling her if it were so. Ida Sentner was not given to bearing her trials in silence.

Had it not been for Josephine's assistance, Tom Sentner's family would have stood an excellent chance of starvation. Josephine practically kept them, and her generosity never failed or stinted. She fed and clothed her nephews and nieces, and all the gray socks whose destination puzzled David so much went to the Sentners.

As for Josephine herself, she had a good farm, a comfortable house, a plump bank account, and was an independent, unworried woman. And yet, in the face of all this, Mrs. Tom Sentner could bewail the fact that Josephine had no husband to look out for her. Josephine shrugged her shoulders and gave up the conundrum, merely saying ironically, in reply to her sister's remark:

"And go to live with Zillah Hartley?"

"You know very well you wouldn't have to do that. Ever since John Hartley's wife at the Creek died he's been wanting Zillah to go and keep house for him, and if David got married Zillah'd go quick. Catch her staying there if you were mistress! And David has such a beautiful house! It's ten times finer than yours, though I don't deny yours is comfortable. And his farm is the best in Meadowby and joins yours. Think what a beautiful property they'd make together. You're all right now, Josephine, but what will you do when you get old and have nobody to take care of you? I declare the thought worries me at night till I can't sleep."

"I should have thought you had enough worries of your own to keep you awake at nights without taking over any of mine," said Josephine drily. "As for old age, it's a good ways off for me yet. When your Jack gets old enough to have some sense he can come here and live with me. But I'm not going to marry David Hartley, you can depend on that, Ida, my dear. I wish you could have heard him rhyming off that poetry last night. It doesn't seem to matter much what piece he recites—first thing that comes into his head, I reckon. I remember one time he went clean through that hymn beginning, 'Hark from the tombs a doleful sound,' and two years ago it was 'To Mary in Heaven,' as lackadaisical as you please. I never had such a time to keep from laughing, but I managed it, for

I wouldn't hurt his feelings for the world. No, I haven't any intention of marrying anybody, but if I had it wouldn't be dear old sentimental, easy-going David."

Mrs. Tom thumped a plucked goose down on the bench with an expression which said that she, for one, wasn't going to waste any more words on an idiot. Easy-going, indeed! Did Josephine consider that a drawback?

Mrs. Tom sighed. If Josephine, she thought, had put up with Tom Sentner's tempers for fifteen years she would know how to appreciate a good-natured man at his real value.

The cold snap which had set in on the day of David's call lasted and deepened for a week. On Saturday evening, when Mrs. Tom came down for a jug of cream, the mercury of the little thermometer thumping against Josephine's porch was below zero. The gulf was no longer blue, but white with ice. Everything outdoors was crackling and snapping. Inside Josephine had kept roaring fires all through the house but the only place really warm was the kitchen.

"Wrap your head up well, Ida," she said anxiously, when Mrs. Tom rose to go. "You've got a bad cold."

"There's a cold going," said Mrs. Tom. "Everyone has it. David Hartley was up at our place to-day barking terrible—a real churchyard cough, as I told him. He never takes any care of himself. He said Zillah had a bad cold, too. Won't she be cranky while it lasts?"

Josephine sat up late that night to keep fires on. She finally went to bed in the little room opposite the big hall stove, and she slept at once, and dreamed that the thumps of the thermometer flapping in the wind against the wall outside grew louder and more insistent until they woke her up. Some one was pounding on the porch door.

Josephine sprang out of bed and hurried on her wrapper and felt shoes. She had no doubt that some of the Sentners were sick. They had a habit of getting sick about that time of night. She hurried out and opened the door, expecting to see hulking Tom Sentner, or perhaps Ida herself, big-eyed and hysterical.

But David Hartley stood there, panting for breath. The clear moonlight showed that he had no overcoat on, and he was coughing hard. Josephine, before she spoke a word, clutched him by the arm and pulled him in out of the wind.

"For pity's sake, David Hartley, what is the matter?"

"Zillah's awful sick," he gasped. "I came here because 'twas nearest. Oh, won't you come over, Josephine? I've got to go for the doctor and I can't leave her alone. She's suffering dreadful. I know you and her ain't on good terms, but you'll come, won't you?"

"Of course I will," said Josephine sharply. "I'm not a barbarian, I hope, to refuse to go to the help of a sick person, if 'twas my worst enemy. I'll go in and get ready and you go straight to the hall stove and warm yourself. There's a good fire in it yet. What on earth do you mean, starting out on a bitter night like this without an overcoat or even mittens, and you with a cold like that?"

"I never thought of them, I was so frightened," said David apologetically. "I just lit up a fire in the kitchen stove as quick's I could and run. It rattled me to hear Zillah moaning so's you could hear her all over the house."

"You need someone to look after you as bad as Zillah does," said Josephine severely.

In a very few minutes she was ready, with a basket packed full of homely remedies, "for like as not there'll be no putting one's hand on anything there," she muttered. She insisted on wrapping her big plaid shawl around David's head and neck, and made him put on a pair of mittens she had knitted for Jack Sentner. Then she locked the door and they started across the gleaming, crusted field. It was so slippery that Josephine had to cling to David's arm to keep her feet. In the rapture of supporting her David almost forgot everything else.

In a few minutes they had passed under the bare, glistening boughs of the poplars on David's lawn, and for the first time Josephine crossed the threshold of David Hartley's house.

Years ago, in her girlhood, when the Hartley's lived in the old house and there were half a dozen girls at home, Josephine had frequently visited there. All the Hartley girls liked her except Zillah. She and Zillah never "got on" together. When the other girls had married and gone, Josephine gave up visiting there. She had never been inside the new house, and she and Zillah had not spoken to each other for years.

Zillah was a sick woman—too sick to be anything but civil to Josephine. David started at once for the doctor at the Creek, and Josephine saw that he was well wrapped up before she let him go. Then she mixed up a mustard plaster for Zillah and sat down by the bedside to wait.

When Mrs. Tom Sentner came down the next day she found Josephine busy making flaxseed poultices, with her lips set in a line that betokened she had made up her mind to some disagreeable course of duty.

"Zillah has got pneumonia bad," she said, in reply to Mrs. Tom's inquiries. "The Doctor is here and Mary Bell from the Creek. She'll wait on Zillah, but there'll have to be another woman here to see to the work. I reckon I'll stay. I suppose it's my duty and I don't see who else could be got. You can send Mamie and Jack down to stay at my house until I can go back. I'll run over every day and keep an eye on things."

At the end of a week Zillah was out of danger. Saturday afternoon Josephine went over home to see how Mamie and Jack were getting on. She found Mrs. Tom there, and the latter promptly despatched Jack and Mamie to the post-office that she might have an opportunity to hear Josephine's news.

"I've had an awful week of it, Ida," said Josephine solemnly, as she sat down by the stove and put her feet up on the glowing hearth.

"I suppose Zillah is pretty cranky to wait on," said Mrs. Tom sympathetically.

"Oh, it isn't Zillah. Mary Bell looks after her. No, it's the house. I never lived in such a place of dust and disorder in my born days. I'm sorrier for David Hartley than I ever was for anyone before."

"I suppose he's used to it," said Mrs. Tom with a shrug.

"I don't see how anyone could ever get used to it," groaned Josephine. "And David used to be so particular when he was a boy. The minute I went there the other night I took in that kitchen with a look. I don't believe the paint has even been washed since the house was built. I honestly don't. And I wouldn't like to be called upon to swear when the floor was scrubbed either. The corners were just full of rolls of dust—you could have shovelled it out. I swept it out next day and I thought I'd be choked. As for the pantry—well, the less said about *that* the better. And it's the same all through the house. You could write your name on everything. I couldn't so much as clean up. Zillah was so sick there couldn't be a bit of noise made. I did manage to sweep and dust, and I cleaned out the pantry. And, of course, I saw that the meals were nice and well cooked. You should have seen David's face. He looked as if he couldn't get used to having things clean and tasty. I darned his socks—he hadn't a whole pair to his name—and I've done everything I could to give him a little comfort. Not that I could do much. If Zillah heard me moving round she'd send Mary Bell out to ask what the matter was. When I wanted to go upstairs I'd have to take off my shoes and tiptoe up on my stocking feet, so's she wouldn't know it. And I'll have to stay there another fortnight yet. Zillah won't be able to sit up till then. I don't really know if I can stand it without falling to and scrubbing the house from garret to cellar in spite of her."

Mrs. Tom Sentner did not say much to Josephine. To herself she said complacently: "She's sorry for David. Well, I've always heard that pity was akin to love. We'll see what comes of this."

Josephine did manage to live through that fortnight. One morning she remarked to David at the breakfast table:

"Well, I think that Mary Bell will be able to attend to the work after today, David. I guess I'll go home tonight."

David's face clouded over.

"Well, I s'pose we oughtn't to keep you any longer, Josephine. I'm sure it's been awful good of you to stay this long. I don't know what we'd have done without you."

"You're welcome," said Josephine shortly.

"Don't go for to walk home," said David; "the snow is too deep. I'll drive you over when you want to go."

"I'll not go before the evening," said Josephine slowly.

David went out to his work gloomily. For three weeks he had been living in comfort. His wants were carefully attended to; his meals were well cooked and served, and everything was bright and clean. And more than all, Josephine had been there, with her cheerful smile and companionable ways. Well, it was all ended now.

Josephine sat at the breakfast table long after David had gone out. She scowled at the sugar-bowl and shook her head savagely at the tea-pot.

"I'll have to do it," she said at last.

"I'm so sorry for him that I can't do anything else."

She got up and went to the window, looking across the snowy field to her own home, nestled between the grove of firs and the orchard.

"It's awful snug and comfortable," she said regretfully, "and I've always felt set on being free and independent. But it's no use. I'd never have a minute's peace of mind again, thinking of David living here in dirt and disorder, and him so particular and tidy by nature. No, it's my duty, plain and clear, to come here and make things pleasant for him—the pointing of Providence, as you might say. The worst of it is, I'll have to tell him so myself. He'll never dare to mention the subject again, after what I said to him that night he proposed last. I wish I hadn't been so dreadful emphatic. Now I've got to say it myself if it is ever said. But I'll not begin by quoting poetry, that's one thing sure!"

Josephine threw back her head, crowned with its shining braids of jet-black hair, and laughed heartily. She bustled back to the stove and poked up the fire.

"I'll have a bit of corned beef and cabbage for dinner," she said, "and I'll make David that pudding he's so fond of. After all, it's kind of nice to have someone to plan and think for. It always did seem like a waste of energy to fuss over cooking things when there was nobody but myself to eat them."

Josephine sang over her work all day, and David went about his with the face of a man who is going to the gallows without benefit of clergy. When he came in to supper at sunset his expression was so woe-begone that Josephine had to dodge into the pantry to keep from laughing outright. She relieved her feelings by pounding the dresser with the potato masher, and then went primly out and took her place at the table.

The meal was not a success from a social point of view. Josephine was nervous and David glum. Mary Bell gobbled down her food with her usual haste, and then went away to carry Zillah hers. Then David said reluctantly:

"If you want to go home now, Josephine, I'll hitch up Red Rob and drive you over."

Josephine began to plait the tablecloth. She wished again that she had not been so emphatic on the occasion of his last proposal. Without replying to David's suggestion she said crossly (Josephine always spoke crossly when she was especially in earnest):

"I want to tell you what I think about Zillah. She's getting better, but she's had a terrible shaking up, and it's my opinion that she won't be good for much all winter. She won't be able to do any hard work, that's certain. If you want my advice, I tell you fair and square that I think she'd better go off for a visit as soon as she's fit. She thinks so herself. Clementine wants her to go and stay a spell with her in town. 'Twould be just the thing for her."

"She can go if she wants to, of course," said David dully. "I can get along by myself for a spell."

"There's no need of your getting along by yourself," said Josephine, more crossly than ever. "I'll—I'll come here and keep house for you if you like."

David looked at her uncomprehendingly.

"Wouldn't people kind of gossip?" he asked hesitatingly. "Not but what—"

"I don't see what they'd have to gossip about," broke in Josephine, "if we were—married."

David sprang to his feet with such haste that he almost upset the table.

"Josephine, do you mean that?" he exclaimed.

"Of course I mean it," she said, in a perfectly savage tone. "Now, for pity's sake, don't say another word about it just now. I can't discuss it for a spell. Go out to your work. I want to be alone for awhile."

For the first and last time David disobeyed her. Instead of going out, he strode around the table, caught Josephine masterfully in his arms, and kissed her. And Josephine, after a second's hesitation, kissed him in return.

Mr. Lismore and the Widow

By Wilkie Collins

Late in the autumn, not many years since, a public meeting was held at the Mansion House, London, under the direction of the Lord Mayor.

The list of gentlemen invited to address the audience had been chosen with two objects in view. Speakers of celebrity, who would rouse public enthusiasm, were supported by speakers connected with commerce, who would be practically useful in explaining the purpose for which the meeting was convened. Money wisely spent in advertising had produced the customary result: every seat was occupied before the proceedings began.

Among the late arrivals, who had no choice but to stand or to leave the hall, were two ladies. One of them at once decided on leaving the hall.

"I shall go back to the carriage," she said, "and wait for you at the door."

Her friend answered, "I sha'n't keep you long. He is advertised to support the second resolution; I want to see him, and that is all."

An elderly gentleman, seated at the end of a bench, rose and offered his place to the lady who remained. She hesitated to take advantage of his kindness, until he reminded her that he had heard what she said to her friend. Before the third resolution was proposed his seat would be at his own disposal again. She thanked him, and without further ceremony took his place. He was provided with an opera-glass, which he more than once offered to her when famous orators appeared on the platform. She made no use of it until a speaker, known in the City as a ship-owner, stepped forward to support the second resolution.

His name (announced in the advertisements) was Ernest Lismore.

The moment he rose the lady asked for the opera-glass. She kept it to her eyes for such a length of time, and with such evident interest in Mr. Lismore, that the curiosity of her neighbours was aroused. Had he anything to say in which a lady (evidently a stranger to him) was personally interested? There was nothing in the address that he delivered which appealed to the enthusiasm of women. He was undoubtedly a handsome man, whose appearance proclaimed him to be in the prime of life, midway, perhaps, between thirty and forty years of age. But why a lady should persist in keeping an opera-glass fixed on him all through his speech was a question which found the general ingenuity at a loss for a reply.

Having returned the glass with an apology, the lady ventured on putting a question next. "Did it strike you, sir, that Mr. Lismore seemed to be out of spirits?" she asked.

"I can't say it did, ma'am."

"Perhaps you noticed that he left the platform the moment he had done?"

This betrayal of interest in the speaker did not escape the notice of a lady seated on the bench in front. Before the old gentleman could answer she volunteered an explanation.

"I am afraid Mr. Lismore is troubled by anxieties connected with his business," she said. "My husband heard it reported in the City yesterday that he was seriously embarrassed by the failure—"

A loud burst of applause made the end of the sentence inaudible.

A famous member of Parliament had risen to propose the third resolution. The polite old man took his seat, and the lady left the hall to join her friend.

"Well, Mrs. Callender, has Mr. Lismore disappointed you?"

"Far from it! But I have heard a report about him which has alarmed me: he is said to be seriously troubled about money matters. How can I find out his address in the City?"

"We can stop at the first stationer's shop we pass, and ask to look at the directory. Are you going to pay Mr. Lismore a visit?"

"I am going to think about it."

The next day a clerk entered Mr. Lismore's private room at the office, and presented a visiting-card. Mrs. Callender had reflected, and had arrived at a decision. Underneath her name she had written these explanatory words: "An important business."

"Does she look as if she wanted money?" Mr. Lismore inquired.

"Oh dear, no! She comes in her carriage."

"Is she young or old?"

"Old, sir."

To Mr. Lismore, conscious of the disastrous influence occasionally exercised over busy men by youth and beauty, this was a recommendation in itself. He said, "Show her in."

Observing the lady as she approached him with the momentary curiosity of a stranger, he noticed that she still preserved the remains of beauty. She had also escaped the misfortune, common to persons at her time of life, of becoming too fat. Even to a man's eye, her dressmaker appeared to have made the most of that favourable circumstance. Her figure had its defects concealed, and its remaining merits set off to advantage. At the same time she evidently held herself above the common deceptions by which some women seek to conceal their age. She wore her own gray hair, and her complexion bore the test of daylight. On entering the room, she made her apologies with some embarrassment. Being the embarrassment of a stranger (and not of a youthful stranger) it failed to impress Mr. Lismore favourably.

"I am afraid I have chosen an inconvenient time for my visit," she began.

"I am at your service," he answered, a little stiffly, "especially if you will be so kind as to mention your business with me in few words."

She was a woman of some spirit, and that reply roused her.

"I will mention it in one word," she said, smartly. "My business is—gratitude."

He was completely at a loss to understand what she meant, and he said so plainly. Instead of explaining herself she put a question.

"Do you remember the night of the 11th of March, between five and six years since?"

He considered for a moment.

"No," he said, "I don't remember it. Excuse me Mrs. Callender, I have affairs of my own to attend to which cause me some anxiety——"

"Let me assist your memory, Mr. Lismore, and I will leave you to your affairs. On the date that I have referred to you were on your way to the railway-station at Bexmore, to catch the night express from the north to London."

As a hint that his time was valuable the ship-owner had hitherto remained standing. He now took his customary seat, and began to listen with some interest. Mrs. Callender had produced her effect on him already.

"It was absolutely necessary," she proceeded, "that you should be on board your ship in the London docks at nine o'clock the next morning. If you had lost the express the vessel would have sailed without you."

The expression of his face began to change to surprise.

"Who told you that?" he asked.

"You shall hear directly. On your way into the town your carriage was stopped by an obstruction on the highroad. The people of Bexmore were looking at a house on fire."

He started to his feet.

"Good heavens! Are you the lady?"

She held up her hand in satirical protest.

"Gently, sir! You suspected me just now of wasting your valuable time. Don't rashly conclude that I am the lady until you find that I am acquainted with the circumstances."

"Is there no excuse for my failing to recognise you?" Mr. Lismore asked. "We were on the dark side of the burning house; you were fainting, and I—"

"And you," she interposed, "after saving me at the risk of your own life, turned a deaf ear to my poor husband's entreaties when he asked you to wait till I had recovered my senses."

"Your poor husband? Surely, Mrs. Callender, he received no serious injury from the fire?"

"The firemen rescued him under circumstances of peril," she answered, "and at his great age he sank under the shock. I have lost the kindest and best of men. Do you remember how you parted from him—burned and bruised in saving me? He liked to talk of it in his last illness. 'At least,' he said to you, 'tell me the name of the man who preserved my wife from a dreadful death.' You threw your card to him out of the carriage window, and away you went at a gallop to catch your train. In all the years that have passed I have kept that card, and have vainly inquired for my brave sea-captain. Yesterday I saw your name on the list of speakers at the Mansion House. Need I say that I attended the meeting? Need I tell you now why I come here and interrupt you in business hours?"

She held out her hand. Mr. Lismore took it in silence, and pressed it warmly.

"You have not done with me yet," she resumed, with a smile. "Do you remember what I said of my errand when I first came in?"

"You said it was an errand of gratitude."

"Something more than the gratitude which only says 'thank you,'" she added. "Before I explain myself, however, I want to know what you have been doing, and how it was that my inquiries failed to trace you after that terrible night." The appearance of depression which Mrs. Callender had noticed at the public meeting showed itself again in Mr. Lismore's face. He sighed as he answered her.

"My story has one merit," he said: "it is soon told. I cannot wonder that you failed to discover me. In the first place, I was not captain of my ship at that time; I was only mate. In the second place, I inherited some money, and ceased to lead a sailor's life, in less than a year from the night of the fire. You will now understand what obstacles were in the way of your tracing me. With my little capital I started successfully in business as a ship-owner. At the time I naturally congratulated myself on my own good fortune. We little know, Mrs. Callender, what the future has in store for us."

He stopped. His handsome features hardened, as if he were suffering (and concealing) pain. Before it was possible to speak to him there was a knock at the door. Another visitor without an appointment had called; the clerk appeared again with a card and a message.

"The gentleman begs you will see him, sir. He has something to tell you which is too important to be delayed."

Hearing the message, Mrs. Callender rose immediately.

"It is enough for to-day that we understand each other," she said. "Have you any engagement to-morrow after the hours of business?"

"None."

She pointed to her card on the writing-table. "Will you come to me to-morrow evening at that address? I am like the gentleman who has just called: I too have my reason for wishing to see you."

He gladly accepted the invitation. Mrs. Callender stopped him as he opened the door for her.

"Shall I offend you," she said, "if I ask a strange question before I go? I have a better motive, mind, than mere curiosity. Are you married?"

"No."

"Forgive me again," she resumed. "At my age you cannot possibly misunderstand me; and yet—"

She hesitated. Mr. Lismore tried to give her confidence. "Pray don't stand on ceremony, Mrs. Callender. Nothing that *you* can ask me need be prefaced by an apology."

Thus encouraged, she ventured to proceed. "You may be engaged to be married?" she suggested. "Or you may be in love?"

He found it impossible to conceal his surprise, but he answered without hesitation.

"There is no such bright prospect in *my* life," he said. "I am not even in love."

She left him with a little sigh. It sounded like a sigh of relief.

Ernest Lismore was thoroughly puzzled. What could be the old lady's object in ascertaining that he was still free from a matrimonial engagement? If the idea had occurred to him in time he might have alluded to her domestic life, and might have asked if she had children. With a little tact he might have discovered more than this. She had described her feeling toward him as passing the ordinary limits of gratitude, and she was evidently rich enough to be above the imputation of a mercenary motive. Did she propose to brighten those dreary prospects to which he had alluded in speaking of his own life? When he presented himself at her house the next evening would she introduce him to a charming daughter?

He smiled as the idea occurred to him. "An appropriate time to be thinking of my chances of marriage!" he said to himself. "In another month I may be a ruined man."

The gentleman who had so urgently requested an interview was a devoted friend, who had obtained a means of helping Ernest at a serious crisis in his affairs.

It had been truly reported that he was in a position of pecuniary embarrassment, owing to the failure of a mercantile house with which he had been intimately connected. Whispers affecting his own solvency had followed on the bankruptcy of the firm. He had already endeavoured to obtain advances of money on the usual conditions, and had been met by excuses for delay. His friend had now arrived with a letter of introduction to a capitalist, well known in commercial circles for his daring speculations and for his great wealth.

Looking at the letter, Ernest observed that the envelope was sealed. In spite of that ominous innovation on established usage in cases of personal introduction, he presented the letter. On this occasion he was not put off with excuses. The capitalist flatly declined to discount Mr. Lismore's bills unless they were backed by responsible names.

Ernest made a last effort.

He applied for help to two mercantile men whom he had assisted in *their* difficulties, and whose names would have satisfied the money-lender. They were most sincerely sorry, but they too refused.

The one security that he could offer was open, it must be owned, to serious objections on the score of risk. He wanted an advance of twenty thousand pounds, secured on a homeward-bound ship and cargo. But the vessel was not insured, and at that stormy season she was already more than a month overdue. Could grateful colleagues be blamed if they forgot their obligations when they were asked to offer pecuniary help to a merchant in this situation? Ernest returned to his office without money and without credit.

A man threatened by ruin is in no state of mind to keep an engagement at a lady's tea-table. Ernest sent a letter of apology to Mrs. Callender, alleging extreme pressure of business as the excuse for breaking his engagement.

"Am I to wait for an answer, sir?" the messenger asked.

"No; you are merely to leave the letter."

In an hour's time, to Ernest's astonishment, the messenger returned with a reply.

"The lady was just going out, sir, when I rang at the door," he explained, "and she took the letter from me herself. She didn't appear to know your handwriting, and she asked me who I came from. When I mentioned your name I was ordered to wait."

Ernest opened the letter.

"DEAR MR. LISMORE: One of us must speak out, and your letter of apology forces me to be that one. If you are really so proud and so distrustful as you seem to be, I shall offend you; if not, I shall prove myself to be your friend.

"Your excuse is 'pressure of business'; the truth (as I have good reason to believe) is 'want of money.' I heard a stranger at that public meeting say that you were seriously embarrassed by some failure in the City.

"Let me tell you what my own pecuniary position is in two words: I am the childless widow of a rich man—"

Ernest paused. His anticipated discovery of Mrs. Callender's "charming daughter" was in his mind for the moment. "That little romance must return to the world of dreams," he thought, and went on with the letter.

"After what I owe to you, I don't regard it as repaying an obligation; I consider myself as merely performing a duty when I offer to assist you by a loan of money.

"Wait a little before you throw my letter into the waste-paper basket.

"Circumstances (which it is impossible for me to mention before we meet) put it out of my power to help you—unless I attach to my most sincere offer of service a very unusual and very embarrassing condition. If you are on the brink of ruin that misfortune will plead my excuse—and your excuse too, if you accept the loan on my terms. In any case, I rely on the sympathy and forbearance of the man to whom I owe my life.

"After what I have now written, there is only one thing to add: I beg to decline accepting your excuses, and I shall expect to see you to-morrow evening, as we arranged. I am an obstinate old woman, but I am also your faithful friend and servant,

"MARY CALLENDER."

Ernest looked up from the letter. "What can this possibly mean?" he wondered.

But he was too sensible a man to be content with wondering; he decided on keeping his engagement.

What Dr. Johnson called "the insolence of wealth" appears far more frequently in the houses of the rich than in the manners of the rich. The reason is plain enough. Personal ostentation is, in the very nature of it, ridiculous; but the ostentation which exhibits magnificent pictures, priceless china, and splendid furniture, can purchase good taste to guide it, and can assert itself without affording the smallest opening for a word of depreciation or a look of contempt. If I am worth a million of money, and if I am dying to show it, I don't ask you to look at me, I ask you to look at my house.

Keeping his engagement with Mrs. Callender, Ernest discovered that riches might be lavishly and yet modestly used.

In crossing the hall and ascending the stairs, look where he might, his notice was insensibly won by proofs of the taste which is not to be purchased, and the wealth which uses, but never exhibits, its purse. Conducted by a man-servant to the landing on the first floor, he found a maid at the door of the boudoir waiting to announce him. Mrs. Callender advanced to welcome her guest, in a simple evening dress, perfectly suited to her age. All that had looked worn and faded in her fine face by daylight was now softly obscured by shaded lamps. Objects of beauty surrounded her, which glowed with subdued radiance from their background of sober colour.

The influence of appearances is the strongest of all outward influences, while it lasts. For the moment the scene produced its impression on Ernest, in spite of the terrible anxieties which consumed him. Mrs. Callender in his office was a woman who had stepped out of her appropriate sphere. Mrs. Callender in her own house was a woman who had risen to a new place in his estimation.

"I am afraid you don't thank me for forcing you to keep your engagement," she said, with her friendly tones and her pleasant smile.

"Indeed I do thank you," he replied. "Your beautiful house and your gracious welcome have persuaded me into forgetting my troubles—for a while."

The smile passed away from her face. "Then it is true," she said, gravely.

"Only too true."

She led him to a seat beside her, and waited to speak again until her maid had brought in the tea.

"Have you read my letter in the same friendly spirit in which I wrote it? "she asked, when they were alone again.

"I have read your letter gratefully, but—"

"But you don't know yet what I have to say. Let us understand each other before we make any objections on either side. Will you tell me what your present position is—at its worst? I can, and will, speak plainly when my turn comes, if you will honour me with your confidence. Not if it distresses you," she added, observing him attentively. He was ashamed of his hesitation, and he made amends for it.

"Do you thoroughly understand me?" he asked, when the whole truth had been laid before her without reserve.

She summed up the result in her own words: "If your overdue ship returns safely within a month from this time, you can borrow the money you want without difficulty. If the ship is lost, you have no alternative, when the end of the month comes, but to accept a loan from me or to suspend payment. Is that the hard truth?"

"It is."

"And the sum you require is—twenty thousand pounds?"

"Yes."

"I have twenty times as much money as that, Mr. Lismore, at my sole disposal—on one condition."

"The condition alluded to in your letter?"

"Yes."

"Does the fulfilment of the condition depend in some way on any decision of mine?"

"It depends entirely on you."

That answer closed his lips.

With a composed manner and a steady hand, she poured herself out a cup of tea. "I conceal it from you," she said, "but I want confidence. Here" (she pointed to the cup) "is the friend of women, rich or poor, when they are in trouble. What I have now to say obliges me to speak in praise of myself. I don't like it; let me get it over as soon as I can. My husband was very fond of me; he had the most absolute confidence in my discretion, and in my sense of duty to him and to myself. His last words before he died were words that thanked me for making the happiness of his life. As soon as I had in some degree recovered after the affliction that had fallen on me, his lawyer and executor produced a copy of his will, and said there were two clauses in it which my husband had expressed a wish that I should read. It is needless to say that I obeyed."

She still controlled her agitation—but she was now unable to conceal it. Ernest made an attempt to spare her.

"Am I concerned in this?" he asked.

"Yes. Before I tell you why, I want to know what you would do—in a certain case which I am unwilling even to suppose. I have heard of men, unable to pay the demands made on them, who began business again, and succeeded, and in course of time paid their creditors."

"And you want to know if there is any likelihood of my following their example?" he said. "Have you also heard of men who have made that second effort—who have failed again—and who have doubled the debts they owed to their brethren in business who trusted them? I knew one of those men myself. He committed suicide."

She laid her hand for a moment on his.

"I understand you," she said. "If ruin comes—"

"If ruin comes," he interposed, "a man without money and without credit can make but one last atonement. Don't speak of it now."

She looked at him with horror.

"I didn't mean that!" she said.

"Shall we go back to what you read in the will?" he suggested.

"Yes—if you will give me a minute to compose myself."

In less than the minute she had asked for, Mrs. Callender was calm enough to go on.

"I now possess what is called a life-interest in my husband's fortune," she said. "The money is to be divided, at my death, among charitable institutions; excepting a certain event—"

"Which is provided for in the will?" Ernest added, helping her to go on.

"Yes. I am to be absolute mistress of the whole of the four hundred thousand pounds—" her voice dropped, and her eyes looked away from him as she spoke the next words—"on this one condition, that I marry again."

He looked at her in amazement.

"Surely I have mistaken you," he said. "You mean on this one condition, that you do not marry again?"

"No, Mr. Lismore; I mean exactly what I have said. You now know that the recovery of your credit and your peace of mind rests entirely with yourself."

After a moment of reflection he took her hand and raised it respectfully to his lips. "You are a noble woman!" he said.

She made no reply. With drooping head and downcast eyes she waited for his decision. He accepted his responsibility.

"I must not, and dare not, think of the hardship of my own position," he said; "I owe it to you to speak without reference to the future that may be in store for me. No man can be worthy of the sacrifice which your generous forgetfulness of yourself is willing to make. I respect you; I admire you; I thank you with my whole heart. Leave me to my fate, Mrs. Callender—and let me go."

He rose. She stopped him by a gesture.

"A young woman," she answered, "would shrink from saying— what I, as an old woman, mean to say now. I refuse to leave you to your fate. I ask you to prove that you respect me, admire me, and thank me with your whole heart. Take one day to think—and let me hear the result. You promise me this?"

He promised. "Now go," she said.

Next morning Ernest received a letter from Mrs. Callender. She wrote to him as follows:

"There are some considerations which I ought to have mentioned yesterday evening, before you left my house.

"I ought to have reminded you—if you consent to reconsider your decision—that the circumstances do not require you to pledge yourself to me absolutely.

"At my age, I can with perfect propriety assure you that I regard our marriage simply and solely as a formality which we must fulfill, if I am to carry out my intention of standing between you and ruin.

"Therefore—if the missing ship appears in time, the only reason for the marriage is at an end. We shall be as good friends as ever; without the encumbrance of a formal tie to bind us.

"In the other event, I should ask you to submit to certain restrictions, which, remembering my position, you will understand and excuse.

"We are to live together, it is unnecessary to say, as mother and son. The marriage ceremony is to be strictly private, and you are so to arrange our affairs that, immediately afterward, we leave England for any foreign place which you prefer. Some of my friends, and (perhaps) some of your friends, will certainly misinterpret our motives, if we stay in our own country, in a manner which would be unendurable to a woman like me.

"As to our future lives, I have the most perfect confidence in you, and I should leave you in the same position of independence which you occupy now. When you wish for my company you will always be welcome. At other times you are your own master. I live on my side of the house, and you live on yours; and I am to be allowed my hours of solitude every day in the pursuit of musical occupations, which have been happily associated with all my past life, and which I trust confidently to your indulgence.

"A last word, to remind you of what you may be too kind to think of yourself. "At my age, you cannot, in the course of nature, be troubled by the society of a grateful old woman for many years. You are young enough to look forward to another marriage, which shall be something more than a mere form. Even if you meet with the happy woman in my lifetime, honestly tell me of it, and I promise to tell her that she has only to wait.

"In the meantime, don't think, because I write composedly, that I write heartlessly. You pleased and interested me when I first saw you at the public meeting. I don't think I could have proposed what you call this sacrifice of myself to a man who had personally repelled me, though I have felt my debt of gratitude as sincerely as ever. Whether your ship is safe or whether your ship is lost, old Mary Callender likes you, and owns it without false shame.

"Let me have your answer this evening, either personally or by letter, whichever you like best."

Mrs. Callender received a written answer long before the evening.

It said much in few words:

"A man impenetrable to kindness might be able to resist your letter. I am not that man. Your great heart has conquered me."

The few formalities which precede marriage by special license were observed by Ernest. While the destiny of their future lives was still in suspense, an unacknowledged feeling of embarrassment on either side kept Ernest and Mrs. Callender apart. Every day brought the lady her report of the state of affairs in the City, written always in the same words: "No news of the ship."

On the day before the ship-owner's liabilities became due the terms of the report from the City remained unchanged, and the special license was put to its contemplated use. Mrs. Callender's lawyer and Mrs. Callender's maid were the only persons trusted with the secret. Leaving the chief clerk in charge of the business, with every pecuniary demand on his employer satisfied in full, the strangely married pair quitted England.

They arranged to wait for a few days in Paris, to receive any letters of importance which might have been addressed to Ernest in the interval. On the evening of their arrival a telegram from London was waiting at their hotel. It announced that the missing ship had passed up channel—undiscovered in a fog until she reached the Downs —on the day before Ernest's liabilities fell due.

"Do you regret it?" Mrs. Lismore said to her husband.

"Not for a moment!" he answered.

They decided on pursuing their journey as far as Munich.

Mrs. Lismore's taste for music was matched by Ernest's taste for painting. In his leisure hours he cultivated the art, and delighted in it. The picture-galleries of Munich were almost the only galleries in Europe which he had not seen. True to the engagements to which she had pledged herself, his wife was willing to go wherever it might please him to take her. The one suggestion she made was that they should hire furnished apartments. If they lived at a hotel friends of the husband or the wife (visitors like themselves to the famous city) might see their names in the book or might meet them at the door.

They were soon established in a house large enough to provide them with every accommodation which they required. Ernest's days were passed in the galleries, Mrs. Lismore remaining at home, devoted to her music, until it was time to go out with her husband for a drive. Living together in perfect amity and concord, they were nevertheless not living happily. Without any visible reason for the change, Mrs. Lismore's spirits were depressed. On the one occasion when Ernest noticed it she made an effort to be cheerful, which it distressed him to see. He allowed her to think that she had relieved him of any further anxiety. Whatever doubts he might feel were doubts delicately concealed from that time forth.

But when two people are living together in a state of artificial tranquillity, it seems to be a law of nature that the element of disturbance gathers unseen, and that the outburst comes inevitably with the lapse of time.

In ten days from the date of their arrival at Munich the crisis came. Ernest returned later than usual from the picture-gallery, and, for the first time in his wife's experience, shut himself up in his own room.

He appeared at the dinner hour with a futile excuse. Mrs. Lismore waited until the servant had withdrawn.

"Now, Ernest," she said, "it's time to tell me the truth."

Her manner, when she said those few words, took him by surprise. She was unquestionably confused, and, instead of looking at him, she trifled with the fruit on her plate. Embarrassed on his side, he could only answer:

"I have nothing to tell."

"Were there many visitors at the gallery?" she asked.

"About the same as usual."

"Any that you particularly noticed?" she went on. "I mean among the ladies."

He laughed uneasily.

"You forget how interested I am in the pictures," he said.

There was a pause. She looked up at him, and suddenly looked away again; but—he saw it plainly—there were tears in her eyes.

"Do you mind turning down the gas?" she said. "My eyes have been weak all day."

He complied with her request the more readily, having his own reasons for being glad to escape the glaring scrutiny of the light.

"I think I will rest a little on the sofa," she resumed. In the position which he occupied his back would have been now turned on her. She stopped him when he tried to move his chair. "I would rather not look at you, Ernest," she said, "when you have lost confidence in me."

Not the words, but the tone, touched all that was generous and noble in his nature. He left his place and knelt beside her, and opened to her his whole heart.

"Am I not unworthy of you?" he asked, when it was over.

She pressed his hand in silence.

"I should be the most ungrateful wretch living," he said, "if I did not think of you, and you only, now that my confession is made. We will leave Munich to-morrow, and, if resolution can help me, I will only remember the sweetest woman my eyes ever looked on as the creature of a dream."

She hid her face on his breast, and reminded him of that letter of her writing which had decided the course of their lives.

"When I thought you might meet the happy woman in my lifetime I said to you, 'Tell me of it, and I promise to tell her that she has only to wait.' Time must pass, Ernest, before it can be needful to perform my promise, but you might let me see her. If you find her in the gallery to-morrow you might bring her here."

Mrs. Lismore's request met with no refusal. Ernest was only at a loss to know how to grant it.

"You tell me she is a copyist of pictures," his wife reminded him. "She will be interested in hearing of the portfolio of drawings by the great French artists which I bought for you in Paris. Ask her to come and see them, and to tell you if she can make some copies; and say, if you like, that I shall be glad to become acquainted with her."

He felt her breath beating fast on his bosom. In the fear that she might lose all control over herself, he tried to relieve her by speaking lightly.

"What an invention yours is!" he said. "If my wife ever tries to deceive me, I shall be a mere child in her hands."

She rose abruptly from the sofa, kissed him on the forehead, and said wildly, "I shall be better in bed!" Before he could move or speak she had left him.

The next morning he knocked at the door of his wife's room, and asked how she had passed the night.

"I have slept badly," she answered, "and I must beg you to excuse my absence at breakfast-time." She called him back as he was about to withdraw. "Remember," she said, "when you return from the gallery to-day I expect that you will not return alone."

Three hours later he was at home again. The young lady's services as a copyist were at his disposal; she had returned with him to look at the drawings.

The sitting-room was empty when they entered it. He rang for his wife's maid, and was informed that Mrs. Lismore had gone out.

Refusing to believe the woman, he went to his wife's apartments. She was not to be found.

When he returned to the sitting-room the young lady was not unnaturally offended. He could make allowances for her being a little out of temper at the slight that had been put on her; but he was inexpressibly disconcerted by the manner—almost the coarse manner—in which she expressed herself.

"I have been talking to your wife's maid while you have been away," she said. "I find you have married an old lady for her money. She is jealous of me, of course?"

"Let me beg you to alter your opinion," he answered. "You are wronging my wife; she is incapable of any such feeling as you attribute to her."

The young lady laughed. "At any rate, you are a good husband," she said, satirically. "Suppose you own the truth: wouldn't you like her better if she was young and pretty like me ?"

He was not merely surprised, he was disgusted. Her beauty had so completely fascinated him when he first saw her that the idea of associating any want of refinement and good breeding with such a charming creature never entered his mind. The disenchantment to him was already so complete that he was even disagreeably affected by the tone of her voice; it was almost as repellent to him as this exhibition of unrestrained bad temper which she seemed perfectly careless to conceal.

"I confess you surprise me," he said, coldly.

The reply produced no effect on her. On the contrary, she became more insolent than ever.

"I have a fertile fancy," she went on, "and your absurd way of taking a joke only encourages me! Suppose you could transform this sour old wife of yours, who has insulted me, into the sweetest young creature that ever lived by only holding up your finger, wouldn't you do it?"

This passed the limits of his endurance. "I have no wish," he said, "to forget the consideration which is due to a woman. You leave me but one alternative." He rose to go out of the room.

She ran to the door as he spoke, and placed herself in the way of his going out.

He signed to her to let him pass.

She suddenly threw her arms round his neck, kissed him passionately, and whispered, with her lips at his ear, "O Ernest, forgive me! Could I have asked you to marry me for my money if I had not taken refuge in a disguise?"

When he had sufficiently recovered to think he put her back from him. "Is there an end of the deception now?" he asked, sternly. "Am I to trust you in your new character?"

"You are not to be harder on me than I deserve," she answered, gently. "Did you ever hear of an actress named Miss Max?"

He began to understand her. "Forgive me if I spoke harshly," he said. "You have put me to a severe trial."

She burst into tears. "Love," she murmured, "is my only excuse."

From that moment she had won her pardon. He took her hand and made her sit by him.

"Yes," he said, "I have heard of Miss Max, and of her wonderful powers of personation; and I have always regretted not having seen her while she was on the stage."

"Did you hear anything more of her, Ernest?"

"Yes; I heard that she was a pattern of modesty and good conduct, and that she gave up her profession at the height of her success to marry an old man."

"Will you come with me to my room?" she asked. "I have something there which I wish to show you."

It was the copy of her husband's will.

"Read the lines, Ernest, which begin at the top of the page. Let my dead husband speak for me."

The lines ran thus:

"My motive in marrying Miss Max must be stated in this place, in justice to her, and, I will venture to add, in justice to myself. I felt the sincerest sympathy for her position. She was without father, mother, or friends, one of the poor forsaken children whom the mercy of the foundling hospital provides with a home. Her after life on the stage was the life of a virtuous woman, persecuted by profligates, insulted by some of the baser creatures associated with her, to whom she was an object of envy. I offered her a home and the protection of a father, on the only terms which the world would recognise as worthy of us. My experience of her since our marriage has been the experience of unvarying goodness, sweetness, and sound sense. She has behaved so nobly in a trying position that I wish her (even in this life) to have her reward. I entreat her to make a second choice in marriage, which shall not be a mere form. I firmly believe that she will choose well and wisely, that she will make the happiness of a man who is worthy of her, and that, as wife and mother, she will set an example of inestimable value in the social sphere that she occupies. In proof of the heartfelt sincerity with which I pay my tribute to her virtues, I add to this, my will, the clause that follows."

With the clause that followed Ernest was already acquainted.

"Will you now believe that I never loved till I saw your face for the first time?" said his wife. "I had no experience to place me on my guard against the fascination—the madness, some people might call it—which possesses a woman when all her heart is given to a man. Don't despise me, my dear! Remember that I had to save you from disgrace and ruin. Besides, my old stage remembrances tempted me. I had acted in a play in which the heroine did—what I have done. It didn't end with me as it did with her in the story. *She* was represented as rejoicing in the success of her disguise. I have known some miserable hours of doubt and shame since our marriage. When I went to meet you in my own person at the picture-gallery, oh, what relief, what joy I felt when I saw how you admired me! It was not because I could no longer carry on the disguise; I was able to get hours of rest from the effort, not only at night, but in the daytime, when I was shut up in my retirement in the music-room, and when my maid kept watch against discovery. No, my love! I hurried on the disclosure because I could no longer endure the hateful triumph of my own deception. Ah, look at that witness against me! I can't bear even to see it."

She abruptly left him. The drawer that she had opened to take out the copy of the will also contained the false gray hair which she had discarded. It had only that moment attracted her notice. She snatched it up and turned to the fireplace.

Ernest took it from her before she could destroy it. "Give it to me," he said.

"Why?"

He drew her gently to his bosom, and answered, "I must not forget my old wife."

Head and Shoulders

By F. Scott Fitzgerald

In 1915 Horace Tarbox was thirteen years old. In that year he took the examinations for entrance to Princeton University and received the Grade A—excellent—in Cæsar, Cicero, Vergil, Xenophon, Homer, Algebra, Plane Geometry, Solid Geometry, and Chemistry.

Two years later while George M. Cohan was composing "Over There," Horace was leading the sophomore class by several lengths and digging out theses on "The Syllogism as an Obsolete Scholastic Form," and during the battle of Château-Thierry he was sitting at his desk deciding whether or not to wait until his seventeenth birthday before beginning his series of essays on "The Pragmatic Bias of the New Realists."

After a while some newsboy told him that the war was over, and he was glad, because it meant that Peat Brothers, publishers, would get out their new edition of "Spinoza's Improvement of the Understanding." Wars were all very well in their way, made young men self-reliant or something but Horace felt that he could never forgive the President for allowing a brass band to play under his window the night of the false armistice, causing him to leave three important sentences out of his thesis on "German Idealism."

The next year he went up to Yale to take his degree as Master of Arts.

He was seventeen then, tall and slender, with near-sighted gray eyes and an air of keeping himself utterly detached from the mere words he let drop.

"I never feel as though I'm talking to him," expostulated Professor Dillinger to a sympathetic colleague. "He makes me feel as though I were talking to his representative. I always expect him to say: 'Well, I'll ask myself and find out.'"

And then, just as nonchalantly as though Horace Tarbox had been Mr. Beef the butcher or Mr. Hat the haberdasher, life reached in, seized him, handled him, stretched him, and unrolled him like a piece of Irish lace on a Saturday-afternoon bargain-counter.

To move in the literary fashion I should say that this was all because when way back in colonial days the hardy pioneers had come to a bald place in Connecticut and asked of each other, "Now, what shall we build here?" the hardiest one among 'em had answered: "Let's build a town where theatrical managers can try out musical comedies!" How afterward they founded Yale College there, to try the musical comedies on, is a story every one knows. At any rate one December, "Home James" opened at the Shubert, and all the students encored Marcia Meadow, who sang a song about the Blundering Blimp in the first act and did a shaky, shivery, celebrated dance in the last.

Marcia was nineteen. She didn't have wings, but audiences agreed generally that she didn't need them. She was a blonde by natural pigment, and she wore no paint on the streets at high noon. Outside of that she was no better than most women.

It was Charlie Moon who promised her five thousand Pall Malls if she would pay a call on Horace Tarbox, prodigy extraordinary. Charlie was a senior in Sheffield, and he and Horace were first cousins. They liked and pitied each other.

Horace had been particularly busy that night. The failure of the Frenchman Laurier to appreciate the significance of the new realists was preying on his mind. In fact, his only reaction to a low, clear-cut rap at his study was to make him speculate as to whether any rap would have actual existence without an ear there to hear it. He fancied he was verging more and more toward pragmatism. But at that moment, though he did not know it, he was verging with astounding rapidity toward something quite different.

The rap sounded—three seconds leaked by—the rap sounded.

"Come in," muttered Horace automatically.

He heard the door open and then close, but, bent over his book in the big armchair before the fire, he did not look up.

"Leave it on the bed in the other room," he said absently.

"Leave what on the bed in the other room?"

Marcia Meadow had to talk her songs, but her speaking voice was like byplay on a harp.

"The laundry."

"I can't."

Horace stirred impatiently in his chair.

"Why can't you?"

"Why, because I haven't got it."

"Hm!" he replied testily. "Suppose you go back and get it."

Across the fire from Horace was another easychair. He was accustomed to change to it in the course of an evening by way of exercise and variety. One chair he called Berkeley, the other he called Hume. He suddenly heard a sound as of a rustling, diaphanous form sinking into Hume. He glanced up.

"Well," said Marcia with the sweet smile she used in Act Two ("Oh, so the Duke liked my dancing!") "Well, Omar Khayyam, here I am beside you singing in the wilderness."

Horace stared at her dazedly. The momentary suspicion came to him that she existed there only as a phantom of his imagination. Women didn't come into men's rooms and sink into men's Humes. Women brought laundry and took your seat in the street-car and married you later on when you were old enough to know fetters.

This woman had clearly materialized out of Hume. The very froth of her brown gauzy dress was art emanation from Hume's leather arm there! If he looked long enough he would see Hume right through her and then he would be alone again in the room. He passed his fist across his eyes. He really must take up those trapeze exercises again.

"For Pete's sake, don't look so critical!" objected the emanation pleasantly. "I feel as if you were going to wish me away with that patent dome of yours. And then there wouldn't be anything left of me except my shadow in your eyes."

Horace coughed. Coughing was one of his two gestures. When he talked you forgot he had a body at all. It was like hearing a phonograph record by a singer who had been dead a long time.

"What do you want?" he asked.

"I want them letters," whined Marcia melodramatically—"them letters of mine you bought from my grandsire in 1881."

Horace considered.

"I haven't got your letters," he said evenly. "I am only seventeen years old. My father was not born until March 3, 1879. You evidently have me confused with some one else."

"You're only seventeen?" repeated March suspiciously.

"Only seventeen."

"I knew a girl," said Marcia reminiscently, "who went on the ten-twenty-thirty when she was sixteen. She was so stuck on herself that she could never say 'sixteen' without putting the 'only' before it. We got to calling her 'Only Jessie.' And she's just where she was when she started—only worse. 'Only' is a bad habit, Omar—it sounds like an alibi."

"My name is not Omar."

"I know," agreed Marcia, nodding—"your name's Horace. I just call you Omar because you remind me of a smoked cigarette."

"And I haven't your letters. I doubt if I've ever met your grandfather. In fact, I think it very improbable that you yourself were alive in 1881."

Marcia stared at him in wonder.

"Me—1881? Why sure! I was second-line stuff when the Florodora Sextette was still in the convent. I was the original nurse to Mrs. Sol Smith's Juliette. Why, Omar, I was a canteen singer during the War of 1812."

Horace's mind made a sudden successful leap, and he grinned.

"Did Charlie Moon put you up to this?"

Marcia regarded him inscrutably.

"Who's Charlie Moon?"

"Small—wide nostrils—big ears."

She grew several inches and sniffed.

"I'm not in the habit of noticing my friends' nostrils.

"Then it was Charlie?"

Marcia bit her lip—and then yawned. "Oh, let's change the subject, Omar. I'll pull a snore in this chair in a minute."

"Yes," replied Horace gravely, "Hume has often been considered soporific— —"

"Who's your friend—and will he die?"

Then of a sudden Horace Tarbox rose slenderly and began to pace the room with his hands in his pockets. This was his other gesture.

"I don't care for this," he said as if he were talking to himself— "at all. Not that I mind your being here—I don't. You're quite a pretty little thing, but I don't like Charlie Moon's sending you up here. Am I a laboratory experiment on which the janitors as well as the chemists can make experiments? Is my intellectual development humorous in any way? Do I look like the pictures of the little Boston boy in the comic magazines? Has that callow ass, Moon, with his eternal tales about his week in Paris, any right to— —"

"No," interrupted Marcia emphatically. "And you're a sweet boy. Come here and kiss me."

Horace stopped quickly in front of her.

"Why do you want me to kiss you?" he asked intently, "Do you just go round kissing people?"

"Why, yes," admitted Marcia, unruffled. "'At's all life is. Just going round kissing people."

"Well," replied Horace emphatically, "I must say your ideas are horribly garbled! In the first place life isn't just that, and in the second place. I won't kiss you. It might get to be a habit and I can't get rid of habits. This year I've got in the habit of lolling in bed until seven-thirty— —"

Marcia nodded understandingly.

"Do you ever have any fun?" she asked.

"What do you mean by fun?"

"See here," said Marcia sternly, "I like you, Omar, but I wish you'd talk as if you had a line on what you were saying. You sound as if you were gargling a lot of words in your mouth and lost a bet every time you spilled a few. I asked you if you ever had any fun."

Horace shook his head.

"Later, perhaps," he answered. "You see I'm a plan. I'm an experiment. I don't say that I don't get tired of it sometimes—I do. Yet—oh, I can't explain! But what you and Charlie Moon call fun wouldn't be fun to me."

"Please explain."

Horace stared at her, started to speak and then, changing his mind, resumed his walk. After an unsuccessful attempt to determine whether or not he was looking at her Marcia smiled at him.

"Please explain."

Horace turned.

"If I do, will you promise to tell Charlie Moon that I wasn't in?"

"Uh-uh."

"Very well, then. Here's my history: I was a 'why' child. I wanted to see the wheels go round. My father was a young economics professor at Princeton. He brought me up on the system of answering every question I asked him to the best of his ability. My response to that gave him the idea of making an experiment in precocity. To aid in the massacre I had ear trouble— seven operations between the age of nine and twelve. Of course this kept me apart from other boys and made me ripe for forcing. Anyway, while my generation was laboring through Uncle Remus I was honestly enjoying Catullus in the original.

"I passed off my college examinations when I was thirteen because I couldn't help it. My chief associates were professors, and I took a tremendous pride in knowing that I had a fine intelligence, for though I was unusually gifted I was not abnormal in other ways. When I was sixteen I got tired of being a freak; I decided that some one had made a bad mistake. Still as I'd gone that far I concluded to finish it up by taking my degree of Master of Arts. My chief interest in life is the study of modern philosophy. I am a realist of the School of Anton Laurier—with Bergsonian trimmings—and I'll be eighteen years old in two months. That's all."

"Whew!" exclaimed Marcia. "That's enough! You do a neat job with the parts of speech."

"Satisfied?"

"No, you haven't kissed me."

"It's not in my programme," demurred Horace. "Understand that I don't pretend to be above physical things. They have their place, but— —"

"Oh, don't be so darned reasonable!"

"I can't help it."

"I hate these slot-machine people."

"I assure you I— —" began Horace.

"Oh shut up!"

"My own rationality— —"

"I didn't say anything about your nationality. You're Amuricun, ar'n't you?"

"Yes."

"Well, that's O.K. with me. I got a notion I want to see you do something that isn't in your highbrow programme. I want to see if a what-ch-call-em with Brazilian trimmings—that thing you said you were—can be a little human."

Horace shook his head again.

"I won't kiss you."

"My life is blighted," muttered Marcia tragically. "I'm a beaten woman. I'll go through life without ever having a kiss with Brazilian trimmings." She sighed. "Anyways, Omar, will you come and see my show?"

"What show?"

"I'm a wicked actress from 'Home James'!"

"Light opera?"

"Yes—at a stretch. One of the characters is a Brazilian rice-planter. That might interest you."

"I saw 'The Bohemian Girl' once," reflected Horace aloud. "I enjoyed it—to some extent— —"

"Then you'll come?"

"Well, I'm—I'm— —"

"Oh, I know—you've got to run down to Brazil for the week-end."

"Not at all. I'd be delighted to come— —"

Marcia clapped her hands.

"Goodyforyou! I'll mail you a ticket—Thursday night?"

"Why, I— —"

"Good! Thursday night it is."

She stood up and walking close to him laid both hands on his shoulders.

"I like you, Omar. I'm sorry I tried to kid you. I thought you'd be sort of frozen, but you're a nice boy."

He eyed her sardonically.

"I'm several thousand generations older than you are."

"You carry your age well."

They shook hands gravely.

"My name's Marcia Meadow," she said emphatically. "'Member it— Marcia Meadow. And I won't tell Charlie Moon you were in."

An instant later as she was skimming down the last flight of stairs three at a time she heard a voice call over the upper banister: "Oh, say— —"

She stopped and looked up—made out a vague form leaning over.

"Oh, say!" called the prodigy again. "Can you hear me?"

"Here's your connection Omar."

"I hope I haven't given you the impression that I consider kissing intrinsically irrational."

"Impression? Why, you didn't even give me the kiss! Never fret—so long."

Two doors near her opened curiously at the sound of a feminine voice. A tentative cough sounded from above. Gathering her skirts, Marcia dived wildly down the last flight, and was swallowed up in the murky Connecticut air outside.

Up-stairs Horace paced the floor of his study. From time to time he glanced toward Berkeley waiting there in suave dark-red reputability, an open book lying suggestively on his cushions. And then he found that his circuit of the floor was bringing him each time nearer to Hume. There was something about Hume that was strangely and inexpressibly different. The diaphanous form still seemed hovering near, and had Horace sat there he would have felt as if he were sitting on a lady's lap. And though Horace couldn't have named the quality of difference, there was such a quality— quite intangible to the speculative mind, but real, nevertheless. Hume was radiating something that in all the two hundred years of his influence he had never radiated before.

Hume was radiating attar of roses.

II

On Thursday night Horace Tarbox sat in an aisle seat in the fifth row and witnessed "Home James." Oddly enough he found that he was enjoying himself. The cynical students near him were annoyed at his audible appreciation of time-honored jokes in the Hammerstein tradition. But Horace was waiting with anxiety for Marcia Meadow singing her song about a Jazz-bound Blundering Blimp. When she did appear, radiant under a floppity flower-faced hat, a warm glow settled over him, and when the song was over he did not join in the storm of applause. He felt somewhat numb.

In the intermission after the second act an usher materialized beside him, demanded to know if he were Mr. Tarbox, and then handed him a note written in a round adolescent hand. Horace read it in some confusion, while the usher lingered with withering patience in the aisle.

"Dear Omar: After the show I always grow an awful hunger. If you want to satisfy it for me in the Taft Grill just communicate your answer to the big-timber guide that brought this and oblige.

Your friend,

Marcia Meadow."

"Tell her,"—he coughed—"tell her that it will be quite all right. I'll meet her in front of the theatre."

The big-timber guide smiled arrogantly.

"I giss she meant for you to come roun' t' the stage door."

"Where—where is it?"

"Ou'side. Tunayulef. Down ee alley."

"What?"

"Ou'side. Turn to y' left! Down ee alley!"

The arrogant person withdrew. A freshman behind Horace snickered.

Then half an hour later, sitting in the Taft Grill opposite the hair that was yellow by natural pigment, the prodigy was saying an odd thing.

"Do you have to do that dance in the last act?" he was asking earnestly—"I mean, would they dismiss you if you refused to do it?"

Marcia grinned.

"It's fun to do it. I like to do it."

And then Horace came out with a *faux pas*.

"I should think you'd detest it," he remarked succinctly. "The people behind me were making remarks about your bosom."

Marcia blushed fiery red.

"I can't help that," she said quickly. "The dance to me is only a sort of acrobatic stunt. Lord, it's hard enough to do! I rub liniment into my shoulders for an hour every night."

"Do you have—fun while you're on the stage?"

"Uh-huh—sure! I got in the habit of having people look at me, Omar, and I like it."

"Hm!" Horace sank into a brownish study.

"How's the Brazilian trimmings?"

"Hm!" repeated Horace, and then after a pause: "Where does the play go from here?"

"New York."

"For how long?"

"All depends. Winter—maybe."

"Oh!"

"Coming up to lay eyes on me, Omar, or aren't you int'rested? Not as nice here, is it, as it was up in your room? I wish we was there now."

"I feel idiotic in this place," confessed Horace, looking round him nervously.

"Too bad! We got along pretty well."

At this he looked suddenly so melancholy that she changed her tone, and reaching over patted his hand.

"Ever take an actress out to supper before?"

"No," said Horace miserably, "and I never will again. I don't know why I came to-night. Here under all these lights and with all these people laughing and chattering I feel completely out of my sphere. I don't know what to talk to you about."

"We'll talk about me. We talked about you last time."

"Very well."

"Well, my name really is Meadow, but my first name isn't Marcia— it's Veronica. I'm nineteen. Question—how did the girl make her leap to the footlights? Answer—she was born in Passaic, New Jersey, and up to a year ago she got the right to breathe by pushing Nabiscoes in Marcel's tea-room in Trenton. She started going with a guy named Robbins, a singer in the Trent House cabaret, and he got her to try a song and dance with him one evening. In a month we were filling the supper-room every night. Then we went to New York with meet-my-friend letters thick as a pile of napkins.

"In two days we landed a job at Divinerries', and I learned to shimmy from a kid at the Palais Royal. We stayed at Divinerries' six months until one night Peter Boyce Wendell, the columnist, ate his milk-toast there. Next morning a poem about Marvellous Marcia came out in his newspaper, and within two days I had three vaudeville offers and a chance at the Midnight Frolic. I wrote Wendell a thank-you letter, and he printed it in his column—said that the style was like Carlyle's, only more rugged and that I ought to quit dancing and do North American literature. This got me a coupla more vaudeville offers and a chance as an ingénue in a regular show. I took it—and here I am, Omar."

When she finished they sat for a moment in silence she draping the last skeins of a Welsh rabbit on her fork and waiting for him to speak.

"Let's get out of here," he said suddenly.

Marcia's eyes hardened.

"What's the idea? Am I making you sick?"

"No, but I don't like it here. I don't like to be sitting here with you."

Without another word Marcia signalled for the waiter.

"What's the check?" she demanded briskly "My part—the rabbit and the ginger ale."

Horace watched blankly as the waiter figured it.

"See here," he began, "I intended to pay for yours too. You're my guest."

With a half-sigh Marcia rose from the table and walked from the room. Horace, his face a document in bewilderment, laid a bill down and followed her out, up the stairs and into the lobby. He overtook her in front of the elevator and they faced each other.

"See here," he repeated "You're my guest. Have I said something to offend you?"

After an instant of wonder Marcia's eyes softened.

"You're a rude fella!" she said slowly. "Don't you know you're rude?"

"I can't help it," said Horace with a directness she found quite disarming. "You know I like you."

"You said you didn't like being with me."

"I didn't like it."

"Why not?" Fire blazed suddenly from the gray forests of his eyes.

"Because I didn't. I've formed the habit of liking you. I've been thinking of nothing much else for two days."

"Well, if you— —"

"Wait a minute," he interrupted. "I've got something to say. It's this: in six weeks I'll be eighteen years old. When I'm eighteen years old I'm coming up to New York to see you. Is there some place in New York where we can go and not have a lot of people in the room?"

"Sure!" smiled Marcia. "You can come up to my 'partment. Sleep on the couch if you want to."

"I can't sleep on couches," he said shortly. "But I want to talk to you."

"Why, sure," repeated Marcia, "in my 'partment."

In his excitement Horace put his hands in his pockets.

"All right—just so I can see you alone. I want to talk to you as we talked up in my room."

"Honey boy," cried Marcia, laughing, "is it that you want to kiss me?"

"Yes," Horace almost shouted. "I'll kiss you if you want me to."

The elevator man was looking at them reproachfully. Marcia edged toward the grated door.

"I'll drop you a post-card," she said.

Horace's eyes were quite wild.

"Send me a post-card! I'll come up any time after January first. I'll be eighteen then."

And as she stepped into the elevator he coughed enigmatically, yet with a vague challenge, at the calling, and walked quickly away.

III

He was there again. She saw him when she took her first glance at the restless Manhattan audience—down in the front row with his head bent a bit forward and his gray eyes fixed on her. And she knew that to him they were alone together in a world where the high-rouged row of ballet faces and the massed whines of the violins were as imperceivable as powder on a marble Venus. An instinctive defiance rose within her.

"Silly boy!" she said to herself hurriedly, and she didn't take her encore.

"What do they expect for a hundred a week—perpetual motion?" she grumbled to herself in the wings.

"What's the trouble? Marcia?"

"Guy I don't like down in front."

During the last act as she waited for her specialty she had an odd attack of stage fright. She had never sent Horace the promised post-card. Last night she had pretended not to see him— had hurried from the theatre immediately after her dance to pass a sleepless night in her apartment, thinking—as she had so often in the last month—of his pale, rather intent face, his slim, boyish fore, the merciless, unworldly abstraction that made him charming to her.

And now that he had come she felt vaguely sorry—as though an unwonted responsibility was being forced on her.

"Infant prodigy!" she said aloud.

"What?" demanded the negro comedian standing beside her.

"Nothing—just talking about myself."

On the stage she felt better. This was her dance—and she always felt that the way she did it wasn't suggestive any more than to some men every pretty girl is suggestive. She made it a stunt.

> *"Uptown, downtown, jelly on a spoon,*
> *After sundown shiver by the moon."*

He was not watching her now. She saw that clearly. He was looking very deliberately at a castle on the back drop, wearing that expression he had worn in the Taft Grill. A wave of exasperation swept over her—he was criticising her.

> *"That's the vibration that thrills me,*
> *Funny how affection fi-lls me*
> *Uptown, downtown— —"*

Unconquerable revulsion seized her. She was suddenly and horribly conscious of her audience as she had never been since her first appearance. Was that a leer on a pallid face in the front row, a droop of disgust on one young girl's mouth? These shoulders of hers—these shoulders shaking—were they hers? Were they real? Surely shoulders weren't made for this!

> *"Then—you'll see at a glance*
> *I'll need some funeral ushers with St. Vitus dance*
> *At the end of the world I'll— —"*

The bassoon and two cellos crashed into a final chord. She paused and poised a moment on her toes with every muscle tense, her young face looking out dully at the audience in what one young girl afterward called "such a curious, puzzled look," and then without bowing rushed from the stage. Into the dressing-room she sped, kicked out of one dress and into another, and caught a taxi outside.

Her apartment was very warm—small, it was, with a row of professional pictures and sets of Kipling and O. Henry which she had bought once from a blue-eyed agent and read occasionally. And there were several chairs which matched, but were none of them comfortable, and a pink-shaded lamp with blackbirds painted on it and an atmosphere of other stifled pink throughout. There were nice things in it—nice things unrelentingly hostile to each other, offspring of a vicarious, impatient taste acting in stray moments. The worst was typified by a great picture framed in oak bark of Passaic as seen from the Erie Railroad—altogether a frantic, oddly extravagant, oddly penurious attempt to make a cheerful room. Marcia knew it was a failure.

Into this room came the prodigy and took her two hands awkwardly.

"I followed you this time," he said.

"Oh!"

"I want you to marry me," he said.

Her arms went out to him. She kissed his mouth with a sort of passionate wholesomeness.

"There!"

"I love you," he said.

She kissed him again and then with a little sigh flung herself into an armchair and half lay there, shaken with absurd laughter.

"Why, you infant prodigy!" she cried.

"Very well, call me that if you want to. I once told you that I was ten thousand years older than you—I am."

She laughed again.

"I don't like to be disapproved of."

"No one's ever going to disapprove of you again."

"Omar," she asked, "why do you want to marry me?"

The prodigy rose and put his hands in his pockets.

"Because I love you, Marcia Meadow."

And then she stopped calling him Omar.

"Dear boy," she said, "you know I sort of love you. There's something about you—I can't tell what—that just puts my heart through the wringer every time I'm round you. But honey—" She paused.

"But what?"

"But lots of things. But you're only just eighteen, and I'm nearly twenty."

"Nonsense!" he interrupted. "Put it this way—that I'm in my nineteenth year and you're nineteen. That makes us pretty close— without counting that other ten thousand years I mentioned."

Marcia laughed.

"But there are some more 'buts.' Your people— —"

"My people!" exclaimed the prodigy ferociously. "My people tried to make a monstrosity out of me." His face grew quite crimson at the enormity of what he was going to say. "My people can go way back and sit down!"

"My heavens!" cried Marcia in alarm. "All that? On tacks, I suppose."

"Tacks—yes," he agreed wildly—"on anything. The more I think of how they allowed me to become a little dried-up mummy— —"

"What makes you thank you're that?" asked Marcia quietly—"me?"

"Yes. Every person I've met on the streets since I met you has made me jealous because they knew what love was before I did. I used to call it the 'sex impulse.' Heavens!"

"There's more 'buts,'" said Marcia

"What are they?"

"How could we live?"

"I'll make a living."

"You're in college."

"Do you think I care anything about taking a Master of Arts degree?"

"You want to be Master of Me, hey?"

"Yes! What? I mean, no!"

Marcia laughed, and crossing swiftly over sat in his lap. He put his arm round her wildly and implanted the vestige of a kiss somewhere near her neck.

"There's something white about you," mused Marcia "but it doesn't sound very logical."

"Oh, don't be so darned reasonable!"

"I can't help it," said Marcia.

"I hate these slot-machine people!"

"But we— —"

"Oh, shut up!"

And as Marcia couldn't talk through her ears she had to.

IV

Horace and Marcia were married early in February. The sensation in academic circles both at Yale and Princeton was tremendous. Horace Tarbox, who at fourteen had been played up in the Sunday magazines sections of metropolitan newspapers, was throwing over his career, his chance of being a world authority on American philosophy, by marrying a chorus girl—they made Marcia a chorus girl. But like all modern stories it was a four-and-a-half-day wonder.

They took a flat in Harlem. After two weeks' search, during which his idea of the value of academic knowledge faded unmercifully, Horace took a position as clerk with a South American export company—some one had told him that exporting was the coming thing. Marcia was to stay in her show for a few months—anyway until he got on his feet. He was getting a hundred and twenty-five to start with, and though of course they told him it was only a question of months until he would be earning double that, Marcia refused even to consider giving up the hundred and fifty a week that she was getting at the time.

"We'll call ourselves Head and Shoulders, dear," she said softly, "and the shoulders'll have to keep shaking a little longer until the old head gets started."

"I hate it," he objected gloomily.

"Well," she replied emphatically, "Your salary wouldn't keep us in a tenement. Don't think I want to be public—I don't. I want to be yours. But I'd be a half-wit to sit in one room and count the sunflowers on the wall-paper while I waited for you. When you pull down three hundred a month I'll quit."

And much as it hurt his pride, Horace had to admit that hers was the wiser course.

March mellowed into April. May read a gorgeous riot act to the parks and waters of Manhatten, and they were very happy. Horace, who had no habits whatsoever—he had never had time to form any—proved the most adaptable of husbands, and as Marcia entirely lacked opinions on the subjects that engrossed him there were very few jottings and bumping. Their minds moved in different spheres. Marcia acted as practical factotum, and Horace lived either in his old world of abstract ideas or in a sort of triumphantly earthy worship and adoration of his wife. She was a continual source of astonishment to him—the freshness and originality of her mind, her dynamic, clear-headed energy, and her unfailing good humor.

And Marcia's co-workers in the nine-o'clock show, whither she had transferred her talents, were impressed with her tremendous pride in her husband's mental powers. Horace they knew only as a very slim, tight-lipped, and immature-looking young man, who waited every night to take her home.

"Horace," said Marcia one evening when she met him as usual at eleven, "you looked like a ghost standing there against the street lights. You losing weight?"

He shook his head vaguely.

"I don't know. They raised me to a hundred and thirty-five dollars to-day, and— —"

"I don't care," said Marcia severely. "You're killing yourself working at night. You read those big books on economy— —"

"Economics," corrected Horace.

"Well, you read 'em every night long after I'm asleep. And you're getting all stooped over like you were before we were married."

"But, Marcia, I've got to— —"

"No, you haven't dear. I guess I'm running this shop for the present, and I won't let my fella ruin his health and eyes. You got to get some exercise."

"I do. Every morning I— —"

"Oh, I know! But those dumb-bells of yours wouldn't give a consumptive two degrees of fever. I mean real exercise. You've got to join a gymnasium. 'Member you told me you were such a trick gymnast once that they tried to get you out for the team in college and they couldn't because you had a standing date with Herb Spencer?"

"I used to enjoy it," mused Horace, "but it would take up too much time now."

"All right," said Marcia. "I'll make a bargain with you. You join a gym and I'll read one of those books from the brown row of 'em."

"'Pepys' Diary'? Why, that ought to be enjoyable. He's very light."

"Not for me—he isn't. It'll be like digesting plate glass. But you been telling me how much it'd broaden my lookout. Well, you go to a gym three nights a week and I'll take one big dose of Sammy."

Horace hesitated.

"Well— —"

"Come on, now! You do some giant swings for me and I'll chase some culture for you."

So Horace finally consented, and all through a baking summer he spent three and sometimes four evenings a week experimenting on the trapeze in Skipper's Gymnasium. And in August he admitted to Marcia that it made him capable of more mental work during the day.

"*Mens sana in corpore sano*," he said.

"Don't believe in it," replied Marcia. "I tried one of those patent medicines once and they're all bunk. You stick to gymnastics."

One night in early September while he was going through one of his contortions on the rings in the nearly deserted room he was addressed by a meditative fat man whom he had noticed watching him for several nights.

"Say, lad, do that stunt you were doin' last night."

Horace grinned at him from his perch.

"I invented it," he said. "I got the idea from the fourth proposition of Euclid."

"What circus he with?"

"He's dead."

"Well, he must of broke his neck doin' that stunt. I set here last night thinkin' sure you was goin' to break yours."

"Like this!" said Horace, and swinging onto the trapeze he did his stunt.

"Don't it kill your neck an' shoulder muscles?"

"It did at first, but inside of a week I wrote the *Quod erat demonstrandum* on it."

"Hm!"

Horace swung idly on the trapeze.

"Ever think of takin' it up professionally?" asked the fat man.

"Not I."

"Good money in it if you're willin' to do stunts like 'at an' can get away with it."

"Here's another," chirped Horace eagerly, and the fat man's mouth dropped suddenly agape as he watched this pink-jerseyed Prometheus again defy the gods and Isaac Newton.

The night following this encounter Horace got home from work to find a rather pale Marcia stretched out on the sofa waiting for him.

"I fainted twice to-day," she began without preliminaries.

"What?"

"Yep. You see baby's due in four months now. Doctor says I ought to have quit dancing two weeks ago."

Horace sat down and thought it over.

"I'm glad of course," he said pensively—"I mean glad that we're going to have a baby. But this means a lot of expense."

"I've got two hundred and fifty in the bank," said Marcia hopefully, "and two weeks' pay coming."

Horace computed quickly.

"Inducing my salary, that'll give us nearly fourteen hundred for the next six months."

Marcia looked blue.

"That all? Course I can get a job singing somewhere this month. And I can go to work again in March."

"Of course nothing!" said Horace gruffly. "You'll stay right here. Let's see now—there'll be doctor's bills and a nurse, besides the maid: We've got to have some more money."

"Well," said Marcia wearily, "I don't know where it's coming from. It's up to the old head now. Shoulders is out of business."

Horace rose and pulled on his coat.

"Where are you going?"

"I've got an idea," he answered. "I'll be right back."

Ten minutes later as he headed down the street toward Skipper's Gymnasium he felt a placid wonder, quite unmixed with humor, at what he was going to do. How he would have gaped at himself a year before! How every one would have gaped! But when you opened your door at the rap of life you let in many things.

The gymnasium was brightly lit, and when his eyes became accustomed to the glare he found the meditative fat man seated on a pile of canvas mats smoking a big cigar.

"Say," began Horace directly, "were you in earnest last night when you said I could make money on my trapeze stunts?"

"Why, yes," said the fat man in surprise.

"Well, I've been thinking it over, and I believe I'd like to try it. I could work at night and on Saturday afternoons—and regularly if the pay is high enough."

The fat men looked at his watch.

"Well," he said, "Charlie Paulson's the man to see. He'll book you inside of four days, once he sees you work out. He won't be in now, but I'll get hold of him for to-morrow night."

The fat man was as good as his word. Charlie Paulson arrived next night and put in a wondrous hour watching the prodigy swap through the air in amazing parabolas, and on the night following he brought two age men with him who looked as though they had been born smoking black cigars and talking about money in low, passionate voices. Then on the succeeding Saturday Horace Tarbox's torso made its first professional appearance in a gymnastic exhibition at the Coleman Street Gardens. But though the audience numbered nearly five thousand people, Horace felt no nervousness. From his childhood he had read papers to audiences—learned that trick of detaching himself.

"Marcia," he said cheerfully later that same night, "I think we're out of the woods. Paulson thinks he can get me an opening at the Hippodrome, and that means an all-winter engagement. The Hippodrome you know, is a big— —"

"Yes, I believe I've heard of it," interrupted Marcia, "but I want to know about this stunt you're doing. It isn't any spectacular suicide, is it?"

"It's nothing," said Horace quietly. "But if you can think of any nicer way of a man killing himself than taking a risk for you, why that's the way I want to die."

Marcia reached up and wound both arms tightly round his neck.

"Kiss me," she whispered, "and call me 'dear heart.' I love to hear you say 'dear heart.' And bring me a book to read to-morrow. No more Sam Pepys, but something trick and trashy. I've been wild for something to do all day. I felt like writing letters, but I didn't have anybody to write to."

"Write to me," said Horace. "I'll read them."

"I wish I could," breathed Marcia. "If I knew words enough I could write you the longest love-letter in the world—and never get tired."

But after two more months Marcia grew very tired indeed, and for a row of nights it was a very anxious, weary-looking young athlete who walked out before the Hippodrome crowd. Then there were two days when his place was taken by a young man who wore pale blue instead of white, and got very little applause. But after the two days Horace appeared again, and those who sat close to the stage remarked an expression of beatific happiness on that young acrobat's face even when he was twisting breathlessly in the air an the middle of his amazing and original shoulder swing. After that performance he laughed at the elevator man and dashed up the stairs to the flat five steps at a time—and then tiptoed very carefully into a quiet room.

"Marcia," he whispered.

"Hello!" She smiled up at him wanly. "Horace, there's something I want you to do. Look in my top bureau drawer and you'll find a big stack of paper. It's a book—sort of—Horace. I wrote it down in these last three months while I've been laid up. I wish you'd take it to that Peter Boyce Wendell who put my letter in his paper. He could tell you whether it'd be a good book. I wrote it just the way I talk, just the way I wrote that letter to him. It's just a story about a lot of things that happened to me. Will you take it to him, Horace?"

"Yes, darling."

He leaned over the bed until his head was beside her on the pillow, and began stroking back her yellow hair.

"Dearest Marcia," he said softly.

"No," she murmured, "call me what I told you to call me."

"Dear heart," he whispered passionately—"dearest heart."

"What'll we call her?"

They rested a minute in happy, drowsy content, while Horace considered.

"We'll call her Marcia Hume Tarbox," he said at length.

"Why the Hume?"

"Because he's the fellow who first introduced us."

"That so?" she murmured, sleepily surprised. "I thought his name was Moon."

Her eyes closed, and after a moment the slow lengthening surge of the bedclothes over her breast showed that she was asleep.

Horace tiptoed over to the bureau and opening the top drawer found a heap of closely scrawled, lead-smeared pages. He looked at the first sheet:

SANDRA PEPYS, SYNCOPATED BY Marcia Tarbox

He smiled. So Samuel Pepys had made an impression on her after all. He turned a page and began to read. His smile deepened—he read on. Half an hour passed and he became aware that Marcia had waked and was watching him from the bed.

"Honey," came in a whisper.

"What Marcia?"

"Do you like it?"

Horace coughed.

"I seem to be reading on. It's bright."

"Take it to Peter Boyce Wendell. Tell him you got the highest marks in Princeton once and that you ought to know when a book's good. Tell him this one's a world beater."

"All right, Marcia," Horace said gently.

Her eyes closed again and Horace crossing over kissed her forehead—stood there for a moment with a look of tender pity. Then he left the room.

All that night the sprawly writing on the pages, the constant mistakes in spelling and grammar, and the weird punctuation danced before his eyes. He woke several times in the night, each time full of a welling chaotic sympathy for this desire of Marcia's soul to express itself in words. To him there was something infinitely pathetic about it, and for the first time in months he began to turn over in his mind his own half-forgotten dreams.

He had meant to write a series of books, to popularize the new realism as Schopenhauer had popularized pessimism and William James pragmatism.

But life hadn't come that way. Life took hold of people and forced them into flying rings. He laughed to think of that rap at his door, the diaphanous shadow in Hume, Marcia's threatened kiss.

"And it's still me," he said aloud in wonder as he lay awake in the darkness. "I'm the man who sat in Berkeley with temerity to wonder if that rap would have had actual existence had my ear not been there to hear it. I'm still that man. I could be electrocuted for the crimes he committed.

"Poor gauzy souls trying to express ourselves in something tangible. Marcia with her written book; I with my unwritten ones. Trying to choose our mediums and then taking what we get—and being glad."

V

"Sandra Pepys, Syncopated," with an introduction by Peter Boyce Wendell the columnist, appeared serially in *Jordan's Magazine*, and came out in book form in March. From its first published instalment it attracted attention far and wide. A trite enough subject—a girl from a small New Jersey town coming to New York to go on the stage—treated simply, with a peculiar vividness of phrasing and a haunting undertone of sadness in the very inadequacy of its vocabulary, it made an irresistible appeal.

Peter Boyce Wendell, who happened at that time to be advocating the enrichment of the American language by the immediate adoption of expressive vernacular words, stood as its sponsor and thundered his endorsement over the placid bromides of the conventional reviewers.

Marcia received three hundred dollars an instalment for the serial publication, which came at an opportune time, for though Horace's monthly salary at the Hippodrome was now more than Marcia's had ever been, young Marcia was emitting shrill cries which they interpreted as a demand for country air. So early April found them installed in a bungalow in Westchester County, with a place for a lawn, a place for a garage, and a place for everything, including a sound-proof impregnable study, in which Marcia faithfully promised Mr. Jordan she would shut herself up when her daughter's demands began to be abated, and compose immortally illiterate literature.

"It's not half bad," thought Horace one night as he was on his way from the station to his house. He was considering several prospects that had opened up, a four months' vaudeville offer in five figures, a chance to go back to Princeton in charge of all gymnasium work. Odd! He had once intended to go back there in charge of all philosophic work, and now he had not even been stirred by the arrival in New York of Anton Laurier, his old idol.

The gravel crunched raucously under his heel. He saw the lights of his sitting-room gleaming and noticed a big car standing in the drive. Probably Mr. Jordan again, come to persuade Marcia to settle down to work.

She had heard the sound of his approach and her form was silhouetted against the lighted door as she came out to meet him. "There's some Frenchman here," she whispered nervously. "I can't pronounce his name, but he sounds awful deep. You'll have to jaw with him."

"What Frenchman?"

"You can't prove it by me. He drove up an hour ago with Mr. Jordan, and said he wanted to meet Sandra Pepys, and all that sort of thing."

Two men rose from chairs as they went inside.

"Hello Tarbox," said Jordan. "I've just been bringing together two celebrities. I've brought M'sieur Laurier out with me. M'sieur Laurier, let me present Mr. Tarbox, Mrs. Tarbox's husband."

"Not Anton Laurier!" exclaimed Horace.

"But, yes. I must come. I have to come. I have read the book of Madame, and I have been charmed"—he fumbled in his pocket— "ah I have read of you too. In this newspaper which I read to-day it has your name."

He finally produced a clipping from a magazine.

"Read it!" he said eagerly. "It has about you too."

Horace's eye skipped down the page.

"A distinct contribution to American dialect literature," it said. "No attempt at literary tone; the book derives its very quality from this fact, as did 'Huckleberry Finn.'"

Horace's eyes caught a passage lower down; he became suddenly aghast—read on hurriedly:

"Marcia Tarbox's connection with the stage is not only as a spectator but as the wife of a performer. She was married last year to Horace Tarbox, who every evening delights the children at the Hippodrome with his wondrous flying performance. It is said that the young couple have dubbed themselves Head and Shoulders, referring doubtless to the fact that Mrs. Tarbox supplies the literary and mental qualities, while the supple and agile shoulder of her husband contribute their share to the family fortunes.

"Mrs. Tarbox seems to merit that much-abused title—'prodigy.' Only twenty— —"

Horace stopped reading, and with a very odd expression in his eyes gazed intently at Anton Laurier.

"I want to advise you—" he began hoarsely.

"What?"

"About raps. Don't answer them! Let them alone—have a padded door."

The Other Man's Wife

By James Oliver Curwood

Thornton wasn't the sort of man in whom you'd expect to find the devil lurking. He was big, blond, and broad-shouldered. When I first saw him I thought he was an Englishman. That was at the post at Lac la Biche, six hundred miles north of civilization. Scotty and I had been doing some exploration work for the government, and for more than six months we hadn't seen a real white man who looked like home.

We came in late at night, and the factor gave us a room in his house. When we looked out of our window in the morning, we saw a little shack about a hundred feet away, and in front of that shack was Thornton, only half dressed, stretching himself in the sun, and LAUGHING. There wasn't anything to laugh at, but we could see his teeth shining white, and he grinned every minute while he went through a sort of setting-up exercise.

When you begin to analyze a man, there is always some one human trait that rises above all others, and that laugh was Thornton's. Even the wolfish sledge-dogs at the post would wag their tails when they heard it.

We soon established friendly relations, but I could not get very far beyond the laugh. Indeed, Thornton was a mystery. DeBar, the factor, said that he had dropped into the post six months before, with a pack on his back and a rifle over his shoulder. He had no business, apparently. He was not a propectory and it was only now and then that he used his rifle, and then only to shoot at marks.

One thing puzzled DeBar more than all else. Thornton worked like three men about the post, cutting winter fire-wood, helping to catch and clean the tons of whitefish which were stored away for the dogs in the company's ice-houses, and doing other things without end. For this he refused all payment except his rations.

Scotty continued eastward to Churchill, and for seven weeks I bunked with Thornton in the shack. At the end of those seven weeks I knew little more about Thornton than at the beginning. I never had a closer or more congenial chum, and yet in his conversation he never got beyond the big woods, the mountains, and the tangled swamps. He was educated and a gentleman, and I knew that in spite of his brown face and arms, his hard muscles and splendid health, he was three-quarters tenderfoot. But he loved the wilderness.

"I never knew what life could hold for a man until I came up here," he said to me one day, his gray eyes dancing in the light of a glorious sunset.

"I'm ten years younger than I was two years ago."

"You've been two years in the north?"

"A year and ten months," he replied.

Something brought to my lips the words that I had forced back a score of times.

"What brought you up here, Thornton?"

"Two things," he said quietly, "a woman—and a scoundrel."

He said no more, and I did not press the matter. There was a strange tremble in his voice, something that I took to be a note of sadness; but when he turned from the sunset to me his eyes were filled with a yet stranger joy, and his big boyish laugh rang out with such wholesome infectiousness that I laughed with him, in spite of myself.

That night, in our shack, he produced a tightly bound bundle of letters about six inches thick, scattered them out before him on the table, and began reading them at random, while I sat bolstered back in my bunk, smoking and watching him. He was a curious study. Every little while I'd hear him chuckling and rumbling, his teeth agleam, and between these times he'd grow serious. Once I saw tears rolling down his cheeks.

He puzzled me; and the more he puzzled me, the better I liked him. Every night for a week he spent an hour or two reading those letters over and over again. I had a dozen opportunities to see that they were a woman's letters: but he never offered a word of explanation.

With the approach of September, I made preparations to leave for the south, by way of Moose Factory and the Albany.

"Why not go the shorter way—by the Reindeer Lake water route to Prince Albert?" asked Thornton. "If you'll do that, I'll go with you."

His proposition delighted me, and we began planning for our trip. From that hour there came a curious change in Thornton. It was as if he had come into contact with some mysterious dynamo that had charged him with a strange nervous energy. We were two days in getting our stuff ready, and the night between he did not go to bed at all, but sat up reading the letters, smoking, and then reading over again what he had read half a hundred times before.

I was pretty well hardened, but during the first week of our canoe trip he nearly had me bushed a dozen times. He insisted on getting away before dawn, laughing, singing, and talking, and urged on the pace until sunset. I don't believe that he slept two hours a night. Often, when I woke up, I'd see him walking back and forth in the moonlight, humming softly to himself. There was almost a touch of madness in it all; but I knew that Thornton was sane.

One night—our fourteenth down—I awoke a little after midnight, and as usual looked about for Thornton. It was glorious night. There was a full moon over us, and with the lake at our feet, and the spruce and balsam forest on each side of us, the whole scene struck me as one of the most beautiful I had ever looked upon.

When I came out of our tent, Thornton was not in sight. Away across the lake I heard a moose calling. Back of me an owl hooted softly, and from miles away I could hear faintly the howling of a wolf. The night sounds were broken by my own startled cry as I felt a hand fall, without warning, upon my shoulder. It was Thornton. I had never seen his face as it looked just then.

"Isn't it beautiful—glorious?" he cried softly.

"It's wonderful!" I said. "You won't see this down there, Thornton!"

"Nor hear those sounds," he replied, his hand tightening on my arm. "We're pretty close to God up here, aren't we? She'll like it—I'll bring her back!"

"She!" He looked at me, his teeth shining in that wonderful silent laugh. "I'm going to tell you about it," he said. "I can't keep it in any longer. Let's go down by the lake."

We walked down and seated ourselves on the edge of a big rock.

"I told you that I came up here because of a woman—and a man," continued Thornton. "Well, I did. The man and woman were husband and wife, and I—"

He interrupted himself with one of his chuckling laughs. There was something in it that made me shudder.

"No use to tell you that I loved her," he went on. "I worshipped her. She was my life. And I believe she loved me as much. I might have added that there was a third thing that drove me up here—what remained of the rag end of a man's honor."

"I begin to understand," I said, as he paused. "You came up here to get away from the woman. But this woman—her husband—"

For the first time since I had known him I saw a flash of anger leap into Thornton's face. He struck his hand against the rock.

"Her husband was a scoundrel, a brute, who came home from his club drunk, a cheap money-spender, a man who wasn't fit to wipe the mud from her little feet, much less call her wife! He ought to have been shot. I can see it, now; and—well, I might as well tell you. I'm going back to her!"

"You are?" I cried. "Has she got a divorce? Is her husband still living?"

"No, she hasn't got a divorce, and her husband is still living; but for all that, we've arranged it. Those were her letters I've been reading, and she'll be at Prince Albert waiting for me on the 15th— three days from now. We shall be a little late, and that's why I'm hustling so. I've kept away from her for two years, but I can't do it any longer—and she says that if I do she'll kill herself. So there you have it. She's the sweetest, most beautiful girl in the whole world— eyes the color of those blue flowers you have up here, brown hair, and—but you've got to see her when we reach Prince Albert. You won't blame me for doing all this, then!"

I had nothing to say. At my silence he turned toward me suddenly, with that happy smile of his, and said again:

"I tell you that you won't blame me when you see her. You'll envy me, and you'll call me a confounded fool for staying away so long. It has been terribly hard for both of us. I'll wager that she's no sleepier than I am to-night, just from knowing that I'm hurrying to her."

"You're pretty confident," I could not help sneering. "I don't believe I'd wager much on such a woman. To be frank with you, Thornton, I don't care to meet her, so I'll decline your invitation. I've a little wife of my own, as true as steel, and I'd rather keep out of an affair like this. You understand?"

"Perfectly," said Thornton, and there was not the slightest ill-humor in his voice. "You—you think I am a cur?"

"If you have stolen another man's wife—yes."

"And the woman?"

"If she is betraying her husband, she is no better than you."

Thornton rose and stretched his long arms above his head.

"Isn't the moon glorious?" he cried exultantly. "She has never seen a moon like that. She has never seen a world like this. Do you know what we're going to do? We'll come up here and build a cabin, and—and she'll know what a real man is at last! She deserves it. And we'll have you up to visit us—you and your wife—two months out of each year. But then"—he turned and laughed squarely into my face—"you probably won't want your wife to know her."

"Probably not," I said, not without embarrassment.

"I don't blame you," he exclaimed, and before I could draw back he had caught my hand and was shaking it hard in his own. "Let's be friends a little longer, old man," he went on. "I know you'll change your mind about the little girl and me when we reach Prince Albert."

I didn't go to sleep again that night; and the half-dozen days that followed were unpleasant enough—for me, at least. In spite of my own coolness toward him, there was absolutely no change in Thornton. Not once did he make any further allusion to what he had told me.

As we drew near to our journey's end, his enthusiasm and good spirits increased. He had the bow end of the canoe, and I had abundant opportunity of watching him. It was impossible not to like him, even after I knew his story.

We reached Prince Albert on a Sunday, after three days' travel in a buckboard. When we drove up in front of the hotel, there was just one person on the long veranda looking out over the Saskatchewan. It was a woman, reading a book.

As he saw her, I heard a great breath heave up inside Thornton's chest. The woman looked up, stared for a moment, and then dropped her book with a welcoming cry such as I had never heard before in my life. She sprang down the steps, and Thornton leaped from the wagon. They met there a dozen paces from me, Thornton catching her in his arms, and the woman clasping her arms about his neck.

I heard her sobbing, and I saw Thornton kissing her again and again, and then the woman pulled his blond head down close to her face. It was sickening, knowing what I did, and I began helping the driver to throw off our dunnage.

In about two minutes I heard Thornton calling me.

I didn't turn my head. Then Thornton came to me, and as he straightened me around by the shoulders I caught a glimpse of the woman. He was right—she was very beautiful.

"I told you that her husband was a scoundrel and a rake," he said gently. "Well, he was—and I was that scoundrel! I came up here for a chance of redeeming myself, and your big, glorious North has made a man of me. Will you come and meet my wife?"

Afterword

"Happy ending" is a subjective concept. I chose the stories in this collection to reflect that. These stories made me think about what, exactly, constitutes a happy ending, but they are also first and foremost enjoyable and entertaining stories.

The Singing Lesson was included in the 1922 collection *The Garden Party and Other Stories*. Author Katherine Mansfield is one of New Zealand's most famous writers, although she spent most of her too short life in Europe, finally dying of tuberculosis in France in 1923, at the age of 34. I chose this story to open the collection because it has the sort of ending we think of when we think of a love story with a happy ending. As you think more about the story, though, you may find yourself wondering if the ending would still be happy if you could check in on the characters in five years. We can only hope it still would be.

Akin to Love was first published in 1909. L.M. Montgomery is best known for *Anne of Green Gables* and its sequels, but also produced many short stories that exhibit the same flair for character. I chose *Akin to Love* for this collection because it explores how sometimes it takes us a few tries to recognize our happy ending.

Mr. Lismore and the Widow is the oldest story in this collection, having originally been published under the title of *She Loves and Lies* in 1883. Wilkie Collins retitled the story when it was included in his *Little Novels* collection in 1887. The question I ponder when I think about this story is whether it would still be a happy ending if Mrs. Callender was exactly as she portrayed herself at the beginning.

*H*ead and Shoulders may be the story with the least happy ending in this collection. I think, though, if you consider the ending from Marcia's point of view rather than Horace's, the tenor of the ending changes quite a bit. Even if you stay firmly in Horace's view point, I think the ending is not entirely unhappy—maybe there is a twinge of regret for a life that might have been, but the life that actually came to pass is not so bad. F. Scott Fitzgerald is best known for his novels, but as this story demonstrates, he wrote wonderful short stories as well. *Head and Shoulders* was first published in The Saturday Evening Post in 1920, and was included in the collection *Flappers and Philosophers*.

*T*he Other Man's Wife, on the other hand, has a happy ending for all involved. Its author, James Oliver Curwood, was an extremely successful writer in his day, but he has not retained the fame of his contemporary Jack London, although both wrote about similar themes. *The Other Man's Wife* was published in the 1920 collection *Back to God's Country and Other Stories*.

*F*ormatting note: I have retained the spellings and grammatical conventions from the original publications to the best of my ability, except in a few cases where I thought the original usage would confuse or distract modern readers. I have, however, introduced illustrations... and perhaps a few typos. I hope you enjoy the former, and apologize for any of the latter that made it through editing.

About the Illustrations

Title page of *The Signing Lesson*: Outline of a piano, from Pixabay.com.

Interior image in *The Singing Lesson*: Line drawing of a chrysanthemum, released into the public domain by the Pearson/Scott Foresman company.

Title page of *Akin to Love*: Knitting needles and yarn, from Pixabay.com.

Interior image in *Akin to Love*: Tea and muffins, from Pixabay.com.

Title page of *Mr. Lismore and the Widow*: Drawing of a 19th century clipper ship, from Pixabay.com.

Interior image in *Mr. Lismore and the Widow*: Drawing of a man writing with a quill pen, released into the public domain by the Pearson/Scott Foresman company.

Title page of *Head and Shoulders*: drawing of an armchair, released into the public domain by the Pearson/Scott Foresman company.

Interior image in *Head and Shoulders:* Vintage postcard image showing a trapeze show. The image shows The Flying Cromwells performing at Midland Beach, Staten Island, New York. Irma and Paul Milstein Division of United States History, Local History and Genealogy, The New York Public Library. The New York Public Library Digital Collections. http://digitalcollections.nypl.org/items/510d47d9-c030-a3d9-e040-e00a18064a99

Title page of *The Other Man's Wife:* Drawing of a moose, from Pixabay.com.

Interior image in *The Other Man's Wife*: Photograph of a lake in the woods, by Samuel Rohl. Accessed under the CC0 license via Pexels.com.

About the Editor

M.R. Nelson discovered a love of short form writing when two young children and a busy career interfered with her lifelong reading habit. She started the website Tungsten Hippo (http://tungstenhippo.com/) to attempt to recruit other people to her newfound passion, and eventually started publishing short writing through Annorlunda Books, a publishing company that she owns and runs.

The "taster flight" idea originated on the Tungsten Hippo website (http://tungstenhippo.com/tags/taster-flights).

About the Publisher

Annorlunda Books is a small press that publishes books to inform, entertain, and make you think. We publish short books (novella length or shorter), fiction or non-fiction. Our publication criteria are simple: if we like it and it taught us something new or made us think, we'll publish it.

Find more information about us and our books online at http://annorlundaenterprises.com/books/ or on Twitter at @AnnorlundaInc.

To stay up to date on all of our releases, subscribe to our mailing list at http://annorlundaenterprises.com/mailing-list/

Other Titles from Annorlunda Books

Taster Flights

Missed Chances is another Taster Flight of classic stories about love. In each of its five stories, there is a hint of "the one that got away."

Original Short eBooks

Unspotted, by Justin Fox, is the story of the Cape Mountain Leopard, the scientist dedicated to saving these rare and elusive big cats, and the author's own journey to try to see one.

Okay, So Look, by Micah Edwards, is a humorous, yet accurate and thought-provoking, retelling of The Book of Genesis.

Navigating the Path to Industry, by M.R. Nelson, is a hiring manager's advice on how to run a successful non-academic job search.

www.ingramcontent.com/pod-product-compliance
Lightning Source LLC
Chambersburg PA
CBHW032039180726
48284CB00008B/2668